UP
THROUGH
THE WATER

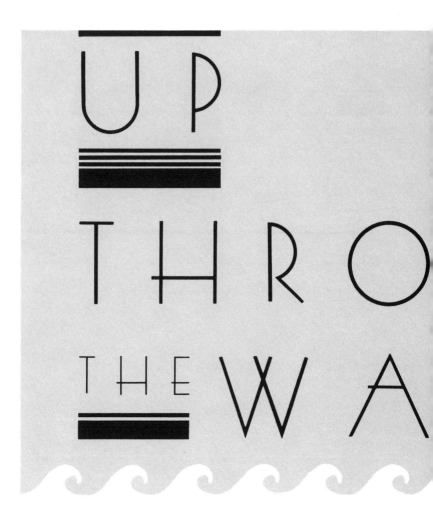

UGH
TER

DARCEY STEINKE

DOUBLEDAY · New York · London · Toronto · Sydney · Auckland

Published by Doubleday, a division of Bantam Doubleday Dell Publishing Group, Inc. 666 Fifth Avenue, New York, New York 10103

Doubleday and the portrayal of an anchor with a dolphin are trademarks of Doubleday, a division of Bantam Doubleday Dell Publishing Group, Inc.

Library of Congress Cataloging-in-Publication Data

Steinke, Darcey.
    Up through the water.
    I. Title.
PS3569.T37924U6   1989   813'.54   88–30877
ISBN 0-385-24687-0

Book Design by Guenet Abraham

Printed in the United States of America

May 1989

FIRST EDITION

TO
PAUL H. PHELPS, JR.

The author would like to thank Jacqueline Kennedy Onassis for her good advice and encouragement. And also Judy Sandman, Craig Mueller, and Paul Ross Leslie for their careful attention to the book.

UP THROUGH THE WATER

JUNE

If you come as most do, down 17, it's around Elizabeth City that the air gets the first sting of salt and handfuls of lost and disoriented gulls circle dumpsters. Then come the ten-shack towns of Camden, Shiloh, Jarvisburg, and Point Harbor, the road between them shaded on one side by low lush woods, green so deep it's nearly black, and big-leafed tobacco plants lined out on the other. Warm blond peaches and watermelon are sold from stands at dusty intervals along the road. The bridge begins at Old Point and four miles later, the car delicately balancing like a high-wire acrobat over Currituck Sound, the outer banks swing out from the coast of North Carolina like the bony curve of a woman's hip. Then the long descent past Duck Beach, then Kitty Hawk where Orville and Wilbur first flew, then Kill Devil Hill where a witch that makes the fish run lives in a shack on the dunes. Down by the arcades and Dairy Queens of Nags Head, past the birdish cottages on stilts in Waves, the road flares out to Avon and Buxton, where on bad days surfers play pinball and check the water every hour for a rise. The zebra-striped lighthouse signals Hatteras and road's end. Farther still the blue smear of the Atlantic and the wait for the boat that will ferry you across to Ocracoke Island.

ONE

MERMAIDS

ike a razor-thin fish she sped to the top, pushed up toward
a light near the surface: a small patch inside the silvery vision
of her eyelids. Even now, as close as she was, close enough to see
clouds beyond the veil of water, she knew she could fall back like a
rock to the dark floor. The tiny ripples of her fingertips grazed the
underbelly of the sea's surface, then broke into air. There was a
kind of slow opening, like sluggish hands working back an orange's peel.

They paused a moment before he rolled them both over to the
night table and picked up his glowing digital watch. His jeans were

slung over the bedpost; he slipped out of bed, pulled them on, and leaned forward so as not to catch himself zipping up. Emily watched him button his shirt and snub out what was left of his cigarette. He looked through the darkness toward her and said, "John Berry will be back soon."

Emily heard Eddie through the walls of the cottage mentioning places she'd never heard of: Twin Falls, HumpBack Mountain, Dragon's Tooth. Once in a while girls' names: Anne, Rachel, Elizabeth. She presumed he knew them from the winter months spent with his father. Eddie murmured again.

"That boy never shuts up," the man said as he pulled his jacket on.

Earlier, at Paolo's she'd been attracted to this man's gray-blue eyes and the way he mulled over his beer. "What's it to you if he talks in his sleep?" The man didn't answer. Emily watched him move away through the kitchen, past the counter, stove, and refrigerator, around the rectangular table. Nearing the door he looked back at her briefly—she was unable to make out his expression—before the screen door rattled behind him.

She felt vibrations in the panel wall, two staggered sounds on the floor, then steps through the kitchen to the bathroom. Emily heard Eddie at the toilet, then the water flushing. He passed by her open door. In the dark he looked like a stick man, his long legs making a simple inverted V. He paused, stared in at her, and then shuffled back to his room. She heard him settle himself in bed. When he was little, she'd check on him, hold a hand over his mouth, always worry it would stay still and dry and she would look closer to see his skin, from his shoulders to where it disappeared beneath the covers, blue and cold as winter stones. But Eddie had stood there, not to see if she was breathing, but to focus his eyes on the pillow near her, to see if there was a man with her in bed.

Emily rolled over to John Berry's side. It was still warm. Half the day and night he worked the ferry traveling back and forth, to and from the cape. She would hear him arrive: thud of the car door, boots on gravel, and then his big frame in the doorway, his mammoth hands already fingering buttons on his uniform. He smelled like the water, and she let her mind see him as a wave moving toward the bed.

He knew nothing yet, suspected nothing. Emily thought—after the first time in May, with the tourist—that he would find out. She'd only spoken a few words to him in a low indecipherable language before they walked a mile down the beach and into the dunes. The winter had been long and boring—but suddenly there they were in the spring, two bodies in the shallow valley the sand dunes made, sea oats crackling around them.

Sometimes she thought it would be a relief to have John Berry find out. It would be easy. There would probably be one tense encounter, which she wouldn't have to initiate, and then he'd leave resolutely, not meandering around the way he might if she suggested separating. She could leave, but the feeling—that any kind of pattern, even a fraudulent one, was better than nothing at all—kept her on. It amazed her that he hadn't heard.

Nearly everyone had heard him at Paolo's. A couple drinks into the night he would start up about Emily and the cottage he would build on the soundside and how they would sit looking out over the water to the thin line of North Carolina, watching the light fade, birds wading long slow mechanical steps in the marshy shore.

She thought of how he slept near her, how he slung his angled arm back behind him, how his shirt would rise on his belly. The slight slope of his stomach seemed vulnerable. His cheeks and forehead were pinker, more vibrant than during the days. His eyelids curved, perfectly shaped like tiny plums.

The door yawned. John Berry's shadow moved around the rectangular table, refrigerator, stove, countertops. He came into the bedroom and threw up the sheet, making it billow for an instant. "Are you awake?"

Eddie said something.

"That kid's been smoking. I can smell it."

She rolled away into a loose oval. He pulled his pants off, got into bed, molded his body around hers, and pressed his knees into the hollow hers made. His arm slipped through the tunnel between her neck and the mattress. Emily could hear blood traversing through his veins. His sea smell collided with her own in the air above their bed like weather fronts.

A few hours later, in the restaurant kitchen, Emily kneaded dough: warm and alive, spreading under her fingers like a man's back.

At first she had waitressed, but after a few seasons it had become hellish, the sneery customers, the way some people ate, her greedy fellow waitresses. And then once, after her fourth season, while explaining a particular sauce to a customer, someone else at the table burnt her with a cigarette. She'd switched to motel work, and the easy order of that had been comforting: clean linens and towels, water glasses in waxed paper bags, each mirror shining under her rag. But it was the repeating and relentless mess of the job that eventually got to her. The last switch, three years ago, was to this kitchen where she did the morning prep work.

The kitchen was still except for the occasional churn of the ice maker and the general hum from the refrigerator. It was T-shaped, with sinks and dishwashers on one end, and stoves, gas ovens, and warmers at the other. The back door was in between. The long part of the T had high shelves for spices and oils, and there were counters for preparation. She stood at one of these now. All the bulk supplies were stored up in the attic. At the foot of the T, the part nearest the dining room, were two swing doors, the big soup heater, and rows and rows of glasses.

Emily'd cut the vegetables. Carrots, zucchini, yellow summer squash swirled like square dancers in the big metal pots near her.

She watched her moving hands in the steel-top table. Above

the stove was a row of smaller glass jars, like the ones her mother had used to store the vegetables and jams. She remembered how one summer a neighborhood boy had explained a trick you could do with a jar. They'd gone to her mother's garden and found a green tomato worm. It was greedily feeding on a ripening tomato, having pinched its way through the taut skin. Its head was inside the mealy meat, eating continuously. When she put her ear very close, she could hear the little thing gobbling with a sound like a sniff, and she had to flick it with one disgusted finger into the jar. She secured the top and put it on a high step by the back. Light glinted into the glass, magnified the midday sun. She watched the tomato worm do just what the boy had said it would. It twitched, spasmed, and began to melt, leaving finally only a soggy circle like mucus. Emily, afraid her mother would see, took the jar to her room, put it under the bed, and lay very still on top of the covers till the coolness hidden in them was gone.

Light was rising outside the restaurant. Objects lost their pleasant blurry bodies and took on definite edges and shapes. When Eddie was very young, she had left him in the front seat of a shopping cart, chewing on a bag of egg noodles. They had been in the frozen foods. She was bending over into the icy canister of frosted orange, dark green for apple and the pink and purple of cranberry and grape. Eddie had whined and shook the hard noodles like a rattle. There was no one in the aisle, and Emily remembered doing something crazy, swinging one leg up and then the next. She laid out on top of the cool cans, cold vapor rising around her. Looking up into the fluorescent lights, she'd seen the section markers like satellites suspended in space and she'd folded her hands over her chest like the dead. She closed her eyes and felt a fine layer of frost forming on her toes. It had been a bag boy, around Eddie's age now, who had finally touched her cheek softly and leaned over into the frozen foods as though to give her a kiss.

Eddie had told her he often dreamt about her, maybe he was dreaming of her now. Underwater, her lips set in a quiet zero, currents moving her dress, showing her body like earth under flowers. She rolled the dough into thin strips for bread, laid them on a greased pan, and put them into the old black oven. When she cracked the door open, her face flushed in the heat.

"How'd you sleep?" she asked as Eddie came in for his morning shift. He stepped into a lemon wedge of light shining through the screen door. Emily reached out to touch his forearm. He jerked away. "Okay," he said, his eyes on his tennis shoes. He wore a sleeveless muscle shirt and gray cotton shorts.

The kitchen crowed with activity: the cook flipped pancakes, it smelled like sausage patties. An older lady sliced melon and pineapples for the breakfast fruit bowls. The waitresses clustered by the swing door.

All morning she stared at Eddie over the sinks. He glanced up through the shelves of spices. Their eyes caught, a look that held, then faltered in slow stares down to their busy hands. She wasn't sure what Eddie thought of her; she wondered how much his father had told him and if he'd heard anything on the island. Earlier seasons she'd presumed he was too young to be bothered by her affairs, but this summer he was definitely noticing and she knew it embarrassed him, made him seem shy.

She watched him rinse plates and line them into the dishwasher. He had his earphones on and his young frame swayed to the rhythm he seemed to feel like a ray of light through his body.

Each day after work, no matter whether there was a falling mist or sun so fierce the water glinted like steel, Emily swam in the ocean. Today the big June sky had dulled. The lifeguard, young, sunbleached, a line of zinc oxide on his nose, read magazines. More tourists would show around one. A few blankets and umbrellas were scattered along the shore. A dragon kite dived and circled, wind-sound on cellophane, its tail a licking tongue.

She threw her towel down, walked into the water, and swam only when she no longer felt the coquina shells on the pads of her feet. She swam parallel to the shore. Each stroke let a million thin swords of pale green light into the water. Emily began rotating, looking out to the horizon, a double feature in blue, sky and water, then face into the sea, bubbles delicately nudging her cheek. Each stroke was something: a faceless baritone voice in the dark, the oleander berries that grew around the cottage, the smell of powder, a baby-blue scarf she used to wear in her hair, the road to the reservoir outside Nashville, Eddie's father spreading a blanket on pine needles, her dress swung over a low branch.

She somersaulted underwater remembering her first night on the island and how she sat on top of the hotel bedspread with hundreds of whitecaps speeding toward her. There had been a print of a boat wrecked against rocks over her head. She remembered lighting white emergency candles when the electricity went out near midnight. And how later she fell asleep against the headboard and woke when drops of wax slipped to her hand. Opening her eyes, she'd seen the flaming wick floating like one boat on clear water and had stared at the ceiling's large opening mouth and remembered Eddie's sleeping face and the angry one of her husband. In the morning, the storm was over and she'd gone out in the clothes she had slept in and walked all the way out to the beach.

Her love of water must have started in the womb, her baby self letting up a few giggly bubbles. Later she could remember someone letting her float in water just slightly cooler than herself. Her mother'd told her she was nearly a year old when her father had held her in the lime quarry near her grandmother's house. For a few minutes he let her splash, her mother said, before Emily had closed her eyes and tried to squirm out of his grasp. Her mother had said the way she fought was the oddest thing she'd ever seen.

Not in a careless baby way but with precise determined movements. From then on she'd always had an understanding with water. She loved to swim in the winter, to be thrashing in the community pool: humidity like a jungle, and the swim teacher, an old water ballet star who still wore a lavender bathing cap with big fluttery scales like a pretty fish. After the lesson she'd returned to the cold where her wet head sent up steam. Years later, Emily and her sister Sarah had paddled a canoe up at Mountain Lake. The water was a dark and earthy green. Leaves and grass treaded and unfurled near her. She saw evergreens and the cool line of water up to them. In high school there were the long baths, the weekly lap swimming at the county's pool where she'd learned flip-turns and stroked evenly from end to end. After she married she swam in the deep water hole where the cows drank. Her husband built her a floating dock and the cows would watch her sometimes, their slow eyes on her as she butterflied and breaststroked and curled underwater.

Emily stopped a moment, treaded. With one foot, she pulled a heavy strand of seaweed from between the toes of the other. She thought of Eddie, how he hadn't said good-bye when she left the restaurant. Each night in the cottage, he turned his cheek to the pillow just as his father had. Both were lively in sleep, speaking riddles, sighing now and then. When she looked in on him, Eddie's mouth was always opened and slack. Often she got close, traced the blond hair on his chest. Daily now, she saw him shyly gaze at her. He meditated on the Gauguin posters of Tahitian women on her walls. Sometimes, flipping his head from them to her as if trying—she imagined—to push her into the South Pacific scenes. This summer his gaze fell always on her as she sunned on the beach near him, or walked from the shower.

Her strokes lengthened: She felt light in the sea, joined to the back and forth pull of the water. Coming together with strangers, dark empty bodies moving on a bed, why did she do it? She asked herself this afterward, in the mornings, sometimes even during, eyes over a muscular shoulder.

Emily swam away from jellyfish, clear floating flowers. She liked her limbs to ache, to nearly buckle with fatigue. She curved underwater, but before she could pull up, a current took her out a few yards. Below the surface she writhed, her hair floated and framed her face. Emily saw a grainy rush of green water, her legs kicked out, and her arms threw punches. John Berry would find out. She swallowed a little water, then came up choking. The sun beat on her hair. She calmed herself and swam on, thinking of the strokes and feeling a firmness inside her body as hard and real as stone.

Dusk. The air was smoky, shadowed with a charcoal pencil. Leaving the beach, she walked in her yellow bathing suit, towel around her head like a turban, up the island road. Dust billowed up from the asphalt in vaulting see-through clouds. Cars passed on their way to the ferry, loaded down with Styrofoam surfboards, mini-sailboats, and beach chairs strapped to the roofs. In worn thongs she found her way over the rocks on the side of the road.

Up ahead, John Berry's truck pulled out from Paolo's lot. She saw it like a child's matchbox car. She would sit beside him in his truck jacked up just enough to see both the soundside and the rolling waves of the beach. Emily might put her head on his lap so John Berry could stroke her hair like he did, his calloused fingertips moving over her face. Way down the beach road, beyond the gas station, beyond the campground, they would park, John Berry's headlights pointed out over the water showing a straight line of lively sea. They would swim together in the ocean, strokes like water ballet girls in perfect sync.

He was ranting the engine, driving fast. Emily focused on his face, his eyes bolting forward, his lips pressed. The truck slammed to a stop a few yards from her.

"I can't believe you!" he yelled.

"What—" she said, but before she could say more she saw the bottle sail from the window, arching up slightly before hitting the fence post near her. It splintered high like water; shards of glass cut her lip, cheek, and chin. Quick blood dripped from her jawbone. She was strangely aware of the sand stuck to the back of her calves and the icy ache at her temple. She saw the small orange sand flowers in microscopic detail at her feet and the sun over the beach sinking into the water. When she looked up, John Berry's truck was way down the island road, its back lights smoldering in a smoke trail that swung back like a gray snake.

His Walkman on, Eddie stood before the metal sink of steamy water. He was mesmerized by the waitresses running in and out of the hot kitchen. They sweated and bitched, picked up trays of Chicken Charles and Seafood Newburg. The backs of their blouses had a white line of wetness down to their skirts. He watched their bodies as they reached for corkscrews, bent for ice, and stole frosting from cakes with one finger. When no one was looking, he sang into the movable water spout. Grabbed it and sneered lyrics from the music. Eddie was letting the dishes soak, having a cigarette, listening to the messy guitar riff pulsating in his ear, and thinking about the fifteen-year-old island girl he'd met on the beach, the one with a body like a real woman.

"Quit the rock star stuff, and get on those soup bowls," the cook said.

Eddie plunged the stacked bowls, crusted with clam chowder, into mountains of bubbles and warm water. This was the day he did the double shift, working from eleven when his mother left till late. "How does it look out there?" he asked the busboy, a skinny kid who ran headlong into the kitchen with the heavy trays. The busboy didn't answer right away; he set down a tray with a thud, then picked through it, looking for a leftover piece of fish or a fragment of cake. Eddie looked disapprovingly at him. The busboy was the only person with a job more disgusting than his own, and besides, Eddie only drank the wine that was left in bottles, carafes, or glasses. Even now he was light-headed, his feet not seeming to rest on the linoleum at all. "Two tables," the busboy said finally, through a mouthful of pink shrimp.

"Thank God," the cook said, and smirked suggestively toward Eddie. He knew that he was worth looking at with his honey-colored tan and hair lightened by the sun. On the beach older tourist women often watched him from under their straw hats. But it was the cook, between sautéing scallops and checking baked fish, who watched inconspicuously as Eddie sang into the water spout. He'd heard the cook liked young boys, and already Neal had suggested a beach ride in his car. He described it all for Eddie: on a blanket under a full moon, passing the champagne bottle back and forth, the calming swish of water around them.

The bubbles tickled Eddie's fingers. He thought how he and the island girl were meeting on Wednesday at Paolo's. She had brown hair, a little like the hair of the one waitress he liked. The waitress was a college girl, tan as wheat bread, who teased him, said he was a punk rocker, and in leaning to pick up an ashtray or a cream pitcher, sometimes pressed her chest to his. For a moment he pictured being with her on the beach under the stars. They'd sip beer and kiss wetly in the roar of the waves.

He dropped a plate.

Quickly taking up a broom, Neal said, "Get your mind off that waitress; she's got herself a college boyfriend." As he swept up the scattered pieces, Eddie saw that he had on black eyeliner. Never on the beach, but sometimes at the island bar, Neal appeared in drag; gold false eyelashes, a silver tear pasted right below his left eye, and earrings that he said once belonged to his mother.

Eddie brushed the white ceramic pieces into the dustpan. He hadn't worked before, and already he could tell it would add a pleasant hang-dog quality to the personality of the summer. His mother had gotten him the job, and yesterday, when he'd come into the restaurant, he overheard her talking to herself while rolling dough into strips: "This one is John Berry," a shortish, thick strip; "This is Daniel," a slightly longer, bent piece; "And this is that tourist who was here last week from Georgia," a thinnish strip like a hot dog.

The owner stumbled in to pick up the petty cash. A fly landed on his sweaty brow, and he picked up the swatter and went after a group of flies by the back door. He swung carelessly, did pirouettes, and finally tried to grab each waitress by the waist as she ran into the kitchen.

"Drunk again," Eddie's waitress whispered in his ear. She shook her head.

Rejected by the girls, he reached for a fly in a spot of old ketchup high on the wall, leaped up, and swung, knocking down a stack of clean dishes.

"Fuck!" Eddie said, hearing the crash and taking off his headphones.

"What did you say?" the owner said.

Eddie was silent. The owner reeled, his belly spilling over his belted jeans. The busboy and Neal watched from their sections of the kitchen.

"What!" the owner screamed right in Eddie's face; his cigarette-liquor breath made Eddie wince.

"Fuck!" he said louder.

"That's probably what your mother is doing right now," the owner said, grinning, spit catching in his beard. After a minute he got the rum for the cakes down from the shelf and left, bent over like a troll, through the back screen door.

Eddie pulled on his blue rubber gloves and put his hands in the warm water.

The cook came over and said, "He's just an old brute."

"I know," Eddie said, looking at the wall, concentrating as if some message might appear there in the dull paint.

"Some people have nothing in the way of manners or respectability, and they don't want you to have any either."

Eddie wanted to respond, but he knew that if he opened his mouth, he would start to cry. He wiped his face on the sleeve of his black T-shirt. Down in the water, his hands felt only the steak knives. It was 100 degrees plus on his side of the kitchen. The metal dishwasher was doing champagne glasses and ice buckets; steam rose from the cracks. The noise and heat that encased him were suddenly soothing, and Eddie's back relaxed.

In Tennessee things were different. His father had a little farm and a new wife. She was small—perfectly formed, but tiny. She canned vegetables: tomatoes floating easily in round jars, peaches in syrup aging to a deep orange. She made wheat bread in even-sized loaves. His father did a bit of farming, but mostly he rented out equipment: yellow tractors and reaping machines. He wore a John Deere baseball cap. Eddie's stepmother taught Sunday school and baked ferociously for church sales. Life with them was easy. They came to his wrestling matches and sat quietly in the bleachers while he struggled on the mat. Afterward, they took him for french fries. Eddie's life had seasons like the two halves of an apple: the calm months with his father and the summer ones here on the island.

The waitress pushed the swing door into the kitchen. "Sorry about that," she said, walking to him.

"It doesn't matter," Eddie said. "He was drunk." If she touched him, Eddie would cry. He felt like the schoolboy who falls at recess whose mother later asks about the bruise on his knee.

"Some stuff should be left alone," she said.

"Yeah," Eddie said, feeling a flutter in his throat, something rising from his stomach like a gray luna moth.

The cook yelled, "Order up, sugar." The waitress turned from the sinks. Eddie watched her gather the entrées on a tray, put a piece of parsley on each, carefully hoist it up to her shoulder, and make her way out the doors to the dining room.

"He should be shot for doing a thing like that to you," the cook said above the whir of fans and dishwashers.

Eddie thought of his mom, tanned dark like an Indian. Sometimes she taught windsurfing on the sound. She screamed instructions at tourists from a little rowboat. Eddie would be riding his bike around the island inlet to the small game room at Paolo's and he would hear her voice faintly over the water. "Terrific. You have it. Maybe steer more with your hands. Lean to the left. You have it. Just go now. Go." Eddie liked the thin lines around his mother's eyes and the fine hairs he could see all over her face in certain light. She knew things about living, about how to live. Eddie liked the posters in her cottage of brown women with fruit baskets on their heads or others with red flowers in their hair. They were round and soft, not like real girls. He saw the scenes warm up and move, his mother among the tropical women. There was one poster over the toilet that he didn't like. Young girls near his own age, but in front of them was this guy with a rust, nearly red beard, and eyes as clear as tap water. Each time Eddie peed into his mother's beige toilet he tried staredowns, gazing into the guy's eyes, waiting for him to blink or flinch.

Eddie walked out to the back porch to have a cigarette, trying to figure out where his mother might be now. The first night spent in her house was always awkward: he tossed and turned, unused to the sand grains which inevitably gathered in the sheets, bothered by the night sounds of katydids and the strong wind off the water. But worse was the fact that she slept, or didn't sleep, in the next room. This season he knew right off when he saw her at the bus station that she was somehow different from before: more restless and flittering. Over a seltzer and lemon at a restaurant, as Eddie told her about the year's happenings in Tennessee, they'd watched the pink beach heather dropping from the glass vase on the table. She brushed the yellow rind with her fingertip and Eddie realized then how much he'd missed her. He'd wanted to tell her how on the bus he watched the wet highway throw up a shine and how with his eyes closed he'd listened to the tires treading in the rain. He wanted to explain how just after midnight, a reading light a few rows back clicked on and he'd seen his outline in the bus window. Two things would happen this summer—his glassy self spoke—you will tell your mother what you think she should do. The lips paused and then smiled—and you will get laid. Now, in Tennessee this would be impossible, for a face to tell you how to act. But in the summer on Ocracoke, things were uneven, malleable, even magic. The reading light went out, the image vanished, and he'd thought of this till the swoosh of the bus wipers sent him again into sleep.

He watched the heat lightning—some flashes, other times thin veins spidering down from the sky. Yesterday at dinnertime he'd been quiet. His mother had told him, "You're a grown man. You should know how life works. I didn't raise you in the dark." She expected him to be tolerant of her ways and he tried to be. But sometimes he felt confused and he knew that then he seemed disapproving.

The moon was edging higher in the already star-bright sky. He'd always thought that his mother was moon and his father sun. Tennessee was the day: definite and bright. His father spoke straight. Chores. School. Wrestling. The island was night: blued with darkness, charged with a wavering mystery below his moon of a mother. Every year was just one day. The long day, always troubled with dreams of the island night. Then summer when at the most incoherent times he held on to Tennessee days.

He was waiting for Neal to bring him the soup pots and baking pans, and heard him putting some into the sink now. He flicked his cigarette into the matted grass behind the restaurant and shivered. Early June, with its blue days and chilly, two-blanket nights, was always his favorite time on the island. There was a feeling of something forming—things coming together so the summer could begin.

As he entered the kitchen, the waitresses were perched on

counters greedily counting their tips; each had a jar with her name on it.

Eddie's favorite waitress went out to the cooler to get jugs of wine to restock the shelf. As he swung open the door, he saw her sitting on two cardboard boxes of crab legs. The cold was a dream. He saw her nude in a block of ice, her body pale and taut, arms outstretched, eyes sleepy. Among the canned pineapples and cold seafood, Eddie knew this was his chance. He could take her, they would lie down, heads resting on the linen tablecloths full of lettuce.

But she wouldn't look at him and he reached for the handle.

"No," she said, stay, it's just that I have to work again in the morning, and I'm so sick of asking people how they want their eggs."

Eddie didn't know how to answer her.

She handed him two large jugs of red wine and she carried two white. "Let's get out of here," she said turning, making a figure eight with her hips.

They were all in the front seat of the white Dodge Dart, upholstery spilling out, crumbling like old pieces of cake on the floor. Green light from the radio. The waitress's shoulders pressed against Eddie.

"I want to see the moon," the waitress said. "Let's stop at the dock."

Neal laughed. "Honey, if the moon is what you want . . ."

As they slowed to a stop, gravel squeezed against the tires. Eddie got out and leaned against the right front headlight. The moon was a capital O in the carbon-paper sky. The waitress sat on the hood, knees to her chest. Her eyes were closed: They were dark and slightly sunken like a blind person's.

"How can you stand it all year?" she asked the cook, who lounged on the front seat, legs hanging out the window.

"You get used to it," he said, a cigarette dangling from his bottom lip.

"You could get used to living in mud," Eddie said. He lobbed gravel from the parking lot into the sea.

The water glittered. Tourist sailboats rocked. He followed a sea gull, just a thin line like a hair on paper.

"This island isn't different from anywhere else," Neal said. "We move around as much as anybody. It's the small things really."

Eddie examined the slack skin of his fingertips; his hands were like an old person's. "The hazards of dishwashing," he said, holding them up, pressing the air flat against his palms.

Neal, his head still resting on the open window frame, tied a red bandanna around his neck. He pulled a joint like a piece of scrap paper from the glove compartment.

The waitress yawned and leaned back against the windshield. "People have no right to say the things they do to one another," she said.

Eddie searched for a smooth flat rock and finally found a thin black one. He looked up to the red moon. No Giants. The water lapped silver. No Mermaids. Just Neal singing an old Stones song with the radio and the waitress getting high on the hood of the car. Eddie walked to the water's edge, slung back his arm, and spun the rock. It jumped one, two, three times, touched the dark water under the moon, and then fell easily, obviously straight down to the bottom of the sea.

In the kitchen Emily sat at the table drinking a rum and coke, the ice cubes clinking like tiny bells. Her face ached, the clotted cuts looked like speckled jam, and black and blues edged up through her skin. The red hole of her cigarette moved up to her mouth, then down to rest on the lip of the clamshell ashtray. The second hand moved like a lazy fluorescent fish on the clock's glowing face. Emily stared again at the refrigerator until it swayed, lost matter, and finally disappeared. She concentrated on the stove, sink, cabinets—willed each gone. Last was the table. It blurred, twitched, vanished. She emptied her glass, eyes falling to the twisted sheets on the bed and then up to the moon.

Each time it was full, she strained her eyes to recognize the crater shapes and letters that were etched on its rocky surface. She always felt, if she could see them, they might be decipherable symbols that would tell her things. She looked into her palm, the lines deepening and ridging, maybe the answers could be read there, but there was no secret in the crosshatch marks and deltaed lines of her hands.

She heard tires on the shell street. Eddie's raspy voice saying good-byes to people from work. He came in the door and carelessly threw open the refrigerator. She turned her face away, a profile against the sharp light, stood, and walked the two steps to him. Bending over into the icebox, she fingered the sliced ham and reached for mustard.

"I'll make you something," she said, her hand to her mouth to hide her sliced lip.

"What did John Berry do to you?" Eddie asked.

"I fell," Emily said, her boozy words muted.

"I'll kill him," he said through his teeth. "That son—"

Emily put her hand over his mouth. Eddie closed his eyes and breathed in as though he was inhaling the sweetest air of his life. She fingered the pocket of his T-shirt. The refrigerator door smacked shut like a wet kiss. He reached out for her, his fingers like a baby's. He placed a hand at the small of her back and held his cheek to hers as if slow-dancing.

TWO

JOHN BERRY

ohn Berry lifted his hand in mock offering of a cracker and
the gulls swooped down. He kept his fist clenched—searching
for the biggest, dirtiest one, the loudest cawer. He sung his other
arm up and aimed the pellet gun, and in a seemingly simultaneous
thud the steel ball left the gun and lodged in the gull's feathered
breast. Blood specks blew on John Berry's arm and face, and the
gull fell quickly into the moving soundside water.

It had been six days since the bottle incident. After it, he had
shot gulls farther out in the marsh. He'd get ten, one every half
hour, and lay the loose birds in the pattern of a cross. But the

afternoon light had made it too easy, and sometimes other gulls flew in patterns at his temples.

He got on a motorcycle parked at the side of the road. The bike was State property, but at the ferry workers' disposal. He pushed hard on the gas; a few sparks scattered as the metal scratched the gravel and he zoomed up the road.

He might decide to do the stunt, but there was no telling until right before—till the tires were rolling on the wood planks and he saw himself flying like some fish, out over the water, then splashing into the sea. The guys had been doing it all summer: driving nearly to the edge of the dock, then turning off the engine, letting the bike fall sideways. The momentum shot them into the air and then down into the water.

John Berry thought he'd do it tonight just for the heck of it, for practice. The power in the bike came into the palms of his hands and up through the bottoms of his feet. He pressed hard on the gas, and leaned into the curve.

Today, like every other, he had worked the ferry securing car tires with wood blocks. It had been hot. He drank shots in the men's bathroom, thinking every crossing tourist knew. There was a vague glow ahead where the docks were. He remembered that year he'd been at college, how he'd come down this road, hands tight on the wheel, his eyes seeing already past everything, right into his parents' cottage and the shells everywhere, the thousands of shells he'd collected since boyhood. They were lined up by size, on the windowsills, on shelves, door frames, his desk, and the most unique were in a big box under his bed, each one wrapped in cotton. Not long after that, he had left again to start a shipping business up in Norfolk with a friend who knew the financial side and had an in on the waterfront. But he'd been unable to tell the hired men what to do. They would sit playing cards and drinking coffee and he would join them. His partner bought him out, gave him a check, and sent him back down this road.

The ferry job seemed perfect. Nearly all the times over, he felt at least a small amount of the initial thrill of going back home, and then, on the way back to the mainland, the simple freedom of being released onto water. It was a connecting kind of job; you hadn't settled for the island, but you weren't off either—you saw more life than most, even if it was in the faces of people crossing. And always you were moving back and forth on the same little bit of sea.

Emily lit up the different corners of his brain. Since Christmas, things had not been right. He was always nagging her not to do laundry in the tub—her bare feet kneading like wine makers'—but off the island at a Laundromat. And he'd seen her eyes drift over the men at the bar. When he dragged the plastic garbage bags to the end of the driveway, he heard the bourbon bottles clink. Sometimes she would stare, tip her head toward the nearest window, and listen as if to check on the sea. She always told him that swimming was the only time she was really happy. He'd figured out that winter what she really wanted was to stay in the water. The way she behaved on land—her languid movements and how she could never be held to a promise—was just a compromise.

A few days ago, he'd picked his way through the scrappy grass and sand stickers and walked down to watch her swim. He'd gone half a mile when he'd spotted her beyond the wake. Her hair was darkened by the water and her face rose every few strokes. Because it was raining, he'd carried a sweatshirt, half hoping she'd come out chilled and he could put it on her shoulders.

That was how it always was—her way out there, doing something, and him just walking along. What made him lonely had been her daily distance, the same space he'd once found alluring. The lovers, those *fucks*, had just made it worse. He knew now that if he hadn't been so angry already, Neal's allusion to her men wouldn't have led to him throwing the bottle. He remembered how the bottle's neck felt snug in his palm. He'd seen it smash and heard splinters belt his car like hard rain. He'd done that because he wanted her attention. John Berry leaned forward into the wind. He realized he would do nearly anything to get her back.

He'd taken her kid, Eddie, out on the road a couple of times. It was awkward, his arms stretched around John Berry's hips and stomach. The kid would whisper in his ear, tickle it as a woman might. He never knew what to say back, and the few times he tried, his words were lost in the wind anyway. Emily encouraged him to do things with her son. The day before he'd found out about Emily, he and Eddie had spiked a watermelon, pouring vodka in gulps out of the bottle. "A Fourth of July tradition," he'd said. "Before long this whole thing will be like one big soaked green olive in the bottom of a martini." The kid had smiled, stepped back, and said something about Emily, still with his father, making martinis, walking around in this special housecoat with a fake fur collar. Eddie was all right. It wasn't that he didn't like him, just that he imagined his own kid, his child with Emily, would be different.

The motorcycle cruised through the long line of numbered ferry spaces, 100 to 99, 98, like counting yourself to sleep. Emily's big four-post bed came into his mind. 75, 74. The white lines and yellow numbers were like frames of movie film: She was waking him because she couldn't sleep: *You don't care whether I sleep well or not* she was saying, the curtains blowing. Her tan leg was hanging out of the covers. He had comforted her as best he could, 42, 41, 40, and the way her face caught every new shade of color in the dawn and how everything had happened so slowly and quietly, 30, 29, 28. The dock, not far ahead, was a takeoff ramp to the night sky, 20, 19, 18. He saw the telephone booth fly by and thought of dialing Emily, letting it ring all night, the sound as constant as the sea in her ears. 10, 9, 8. He revved the bike's engine and stood up a little as his tires bumped onto the boards.

· · ·

The ferry tugged out of the dock. John Berry woke with a start, one of those falling mini-dreams, toppling over and down huge cement stairs. His mouth was dry as a flannel shirt, his clothes damp, and he didn't remember getting from the water to his cot in the engine room.

"Can't live on booze," Tom's voice said from behind. "I brought you some biscuits." He sat down on the metal bench soldered to the wall. John Berry sat up and opened the bag. "You got to get back," Tom said. "You can't stay on the water all summer."

John Berry rubbed his beard, cocked one green eye, and put a biscuit into his mouth. "I have a plan to get her back," he said, looking down at his boots.

Tom walked to the door and shook his head. "We're almost to Pelican. Get up here and unload."

In the men's room, John Berry washed his face, dried it with paper towels, wet his hand, and patted down the wild cowlicks rising like seedlings all over his head.

There was a process crudely called the Trollop Express, in which ferry men, mostly the married ones, had agreed to call the few eligible island men and let them know if any attractive, lonely-looking women were on the winter ferries. The day Emily had traveled over for the first time John Berry heard Tom say that he was calling her in to the boys to get his twenty bucks. John Berry had watched as Emily leaned her stomach against the black rail. She had on a long, ratty, down coat that fell below the hem of her dress. Her legs were bare and on her feet she'd had blue suede clogs. The wind had forced goose bumps all over her ankles and up her calves. She'd held her frenzied hair from her eyes.

"Buddy," John Berry had yelled over the fall of wind. "I'll give you the twenty if you don't—" and he had dialed a phone in the air.

John Berry left the bathroom. The last car struggled onto the deck. He walked through the long alley of car doors. Tourists crowded to the right side to see tiny Pelican Island. The fleshy chins of the birds swaggled. John Berry's eyes blurred as he saw girls in the water, wading waist level—six of them blurring to four and then two. Girls with opaque faces like transparent fish and hair cut close to their heads. They all went under with a flick and glint of metallic toes.

"Aren't they something?" John Berry said to Tom, who stood looking over the water with him.

"The birds?" Tom said.

John Berry bent farther over the chain link fence. He wanted to hear their whispers bubbling up from the water. One swam near the boat, moved in arcs and ovals, and motioned with a shimmy of her shoulders. The boat approached the big island. Tom said, "Why don't you come back with me to Hatteras?"

John Berry turned and Tom's hand slipped from his back. He thought of the beads Emily hung in the bathroom on nails above the porcelain tub. How sometimes she'd wear a string of jade, round green beads nudging her nipples, swinging, reaching all the way down to the fine hairs of her lower stomach. He held a hand up to block the sun; it glinted off the hood of every car, making each a blinding flash—he saw Emily in every back seat kissing a stranger.

THREE

PONIES

Eddie drank some Coke, put on his headset, and listened to his Walkman. Paolo's was the only bar on Ocracoke and because they served food too, pizza and subs, they let underage kids like him hang around. It was a cedar building on stilts just like the cottages on the soundside of the island. Eddie sat at a table near the windows in back. It was his day off and for a while he'd stayed in bed reading a mystery book his father had sent him from home. The hero killed people, but Eddie liked it that the guy always felt bad for a couple of days after. He watched the clock over the bar, waiting for Lila.

Rain hit the roof. Eddie flipped through some postcards, and chose one with ponies running on the front to send to his father. Whenever he heard the door creak or the rain shift against the side of the building, he lifted his head from writing. He couldn't remember seeing Lila last year. Islanders usually stayed away from summer help, even from transplanted year-around residents like his mother. The island girls had always seemed a strange mix, awkward in their oversized boyish clothing and also cocky, having a physical ease that marked them instantly as locals.

Maybe Lila had stood him up. He had trouble making friends in the summers. The island boys were busy with family businesses and the tourist ones always left in a week or two. He picked up a quarter to play another video. The beer man came in wearing a plastic poncho. He wiped rain from his face with two fingers. Eddie turned, not wanting the bartender to know that he was anxious. The door opened again and Lila stepped in. She shook her black umbrella with the bent metal rib and headed for his table. "This stupid rain," she said.

"I thought you might not come," Eddie said, half standing, bumping the table with his hip.

"No reason not to," Lila laughed.

She sat down and stretched her legs under the table and onto the chair across from her. She had on wrinkled painter's pants and a rose blouse, snug around the shoulders. Her face was broad with large eyes and a birthmark shaped like a kidney bean on one cheek. She looked pretty in an odd way.

The silence seemed too long and he fiddled with his cassette case. "You don't remember me from last year, do you?" Lila said, cracking her pink gum.

He didn't know what to tell her. He could remember her, though only vaguely—one of the thin shy girls who hung around the docks at night.

"I saw you once doing push-ups on the beach. Your nose in the sand."

"For wrestling." Eddie tried to laugh. He knew how his face contorted when he exercised. "You said you'd show me the ponies."

"I might," Lila said. "After the rain stops and it gets dark."

The bartender put down sodas and Eddie heard his fizz. "Can you ride them?" he said.

"If you know how," she said, twisting her hair around her finger.

"So you've done it?"

"Sure," Lila said. "At first it seems scary. I've gotten thrown a few times. It's weird; you feel like you're flying, then you smack on the ground. Everything's quiet till the ponies gather around and laugh."

"I think I could ride them," Eddie said. Lila smiled but seemed to ignore him. He'd never seen a girl like her. The high school girls he knew in Tennessee were always combing their hair and giggling over the basketball players. Lila could talk regular and there was something kind of fierce about her.

"Last summer I could fit in my father's crab trap," Lila said. "They used to call me chicken because I was so bony."

"No way," Eddie said, slightly embarrassed.

"This spring I put all my old toys, dolls, puzzles, that kind of stuff, in a box, taped it up, and wrote *childhood* on every side. Clever, huh? It's up in my closet next to my globe."

It seemed a funny thing to admit, Eddie thought, and he watched her stir her Coke with her fingers. He didn't know what to say. "Is the island on that thing?"

"At first I thought it was a little dot like a speck of pepper," Lila said, shaking her head. "But it's not even on there." He thought of the island, the Victorian sea captains' cottages around the inlet and the sea oats that curtained the beach. She leaned her face closer to his. "When I was a kid," she said, "I used to wonder where hell was on globes."

"That's funny," Eddie said. He liked the way her throat trilled when she laughed. She smiled and brought her cheek down close to her shoulder and rubbed it slowly against her shirt. Eddie had a feeling he was watching something private.

The small arcade was separated from the dining room by a half wall and was darker than the rest of the bar. The pinball machine played "Pop Goes the Weasel" in tiny notes, its light concentrated like a camp fire.

There was something about the big blonde dressed like a soldier on the glass back that he liked. She looked similar to the girls in the X-rated comics he'd seen back home and she reminded him of his friends there. The woman was barely clothed, with one leg straddled over her motorcycle. There were rats in uniform around her feet, all grinning so their spiked teeth showed.

Eddie put quarters in the thin slot and the numbers, set inside the woman's chest, cleared to zeros. The silver ball shot down past the motorcycle men with raised clubs. He flipped the ball up and it pinged on a rat with a handgun and then to an army nurse in a short dress. He caught the ball, balanced it on a flipper, and asked if she wanted to take over.

Lila moved her body in back of his, reached her arms around, and pressed down on his fingers resting on the knobs. She flipped the ball back and Eddie ducked under her arms. He leaned against the side of the lighted scoreboard, watching as her eyes narrowed on the game. She pressed right up against the edge. "This machine's been here for ten years. I remember my father telling me those rats were rabbits." Eddie saw her move her neck like a swan bending to water. She missed and the silver ball slid past the flippers and down into the machine's inner organs.

Lila swung the flashlight to the beaten grass around the wooden stakes. "They must be down by the water, grazing in the swamp."

She pulled herself over. Eddie scaled the fence and followed. Light illuminated their feet along the dirt path. Above them the sky was purple-blue with a smattering of stars. He stumbled a little and tried to hide it by bending over to retie his shoe. Now that he was here, he wasn't sure he wanted to ride the ponies. But he couldn't think of any excuse.

They were clumped together. The light made their eyes blink lazily like cows. Eddie'd heard about them for years. His mother had told him that men once wanted them for polo ponies because they were petite, elegant, and strong. He'd caught a few glimpses of them from car windows, their loping manes moving down by the sound, and once the ponies had been grazing by the highway. Their quick retreat had sent up dust so that to him they hadn't seemed real.

"Looks like they're talking," Lila said. Eddie watched her study the blue-gray shades of their fur. "I bet they're talking about the old days when they ran everywhere." Eddie knew the story—they were pirate horses. The only survivors of a shipwreck. Lila pointed the flashlight on a gray mare who whinnied loudly. "See how their backs bow?" Lila said. "My father says that's from scurvy."

She put the end of the flashlight into the sandy earth. Its circle of light immediately drew gnats and tiny white moths. The horses stirred. "We have to sneak up on them," Lila said, squeezing her hands into fists.

"I wish we had some rope," Eddie said.

"You can't tie 'em up; they'd go crazy. Just hold on with your legs."

She put her finger to her lips, grabbed his hand, and they crept to the group of horses. Lila whispered *now* and she ran toward the darkest of the bunch. Eddie's heart pounded in his head as he grabbed the mane of a smaller one and pulled himself over. He'd ridden horses before, but none as lively as these. The horse bucked up, threw its back legs out like a rodeo bronco, and whined as though it had been shot.

"Talk to it," Lila said. She cooed at her own tussling animal. His horse turned its head and tried to bite his leg. "Dig your heels in," Lila yelled. Eddie did this, and the horse eased the struggle and began to run at an awful jumping clip. It wanted him off. He was jerked and the stars in front of him blurred across the sky. "Do you have him?" she yelled back.

"I think so," Eddie said.

Lila steered her horse away. "I know," he heard her say, "I wouldn't want nothing riding me either."

Eddie's pony followed Lila's toward the fence. He listened to the wet hoof sound in mud. She crouched, grabbed deeper into the mane, and gave her horse a sharp kick in the shank. He watched how her body lifted with the horse, heard it humph and then the sound of its hoofs on the grass. His pony was less angry now, cantering toward the fence. Eddie tried to breathe evenly and think how great it was going to be to ride on the beach with Lila.

"What are you waiting for?" she called to him from the other side.

He couldn't see her, just the bare stakes of the pen. "Over," he said and kicked the horse with his heels. It reared back, pitching its front legs into the air.

"Hit it on the neck," Lila said.

He did and the horse tried the fence. Eddie's head burst big red blossoms. He heard the hoof catch and the horse cry out. Then the crunch, the sound of a huge branch snapping: Eddie was falling, breathing the horse, face pressed to fur, head vibrating on the ground. He sprawled so near he could touch the belly and hear its quivering breath. The pony lay just over the railings, body twisted: back right leg stuck between the wooden rungs, front legs bent under, a visible gash at the knee, protruding bone.

"Get up," Lila screamed.

He heard her feet thud on the ground and her horse gallop off toward the beach. Standing, he saw silver minnows on the edge of his vision.

"It's in shock," Lila said.

"We have to get someone," he said loudly, looking toward the dark ribbon of highway and then to Lila. He knew an injured horse would be shot.

"Calm down," she said. The pony blinked a watery eye. "Once it gets light, the birds will eat its eyes out." The animal's breath steadied. Eddie's legs felt shaky, the air around him throbbed.

"Get the flashlight. We'll drag it to the water."

Eddie walked toward the hum of light. He wanted to run hard toward the beach and look back to see the horse sprout wings—thick, feathery, and muscular as a duck's—and fly toward the stars. The faded lights of the sky reminded him of the ovals and longer-shaped cuts that scattered his mother's face—there was something about those cuts, they seemed to hold a charged and tingling energy. And there was something also around the pony that reminded Eddie of his mother. Both threw the same invisible hurt and wobbly arrows. His mother's eye paired, in his head, with the pony's.

"Get over here," Lila yelled to him. He cleared the fence, grabbed the light, then ran back. "Take your shirt off," she said and he pulled the T-shirt over his head. She asked him to hold the light as she tied the shirt around the horse's neck. A thick line of blood ran from the animal's ear. "You pull and I'll push from behind."

The horse made horrible rattling sounds. Its fur scraped in the mud. It thrashed its unhurt leg and swung its head and then grew tired and still, its slack weight like a rock.

During these moments they stopped to rest. Lila stroked its neck and hummed as if putting the pony to sleep. But eventually it would buckle and try to push itself up with its head. Right before the shore, the pony gave a long gravelly moan that made Eddie feel sick. Finally, after what seemed like an hour, the horse's head touched water and its thick tongue lapped.

Their tennis shoes squelched on the shelves and rolls of the seafloor. Lila told him to stop. He pulled on the loose arm of the shirt. The water was at his chest. He was not the greatest swimmer and was worried the horse might somehow pin him under. "Put your hands on its shoulders and stay clear of the back legs," Lila said and moved slowly through the water like a moonwalker. She bent her head down to whisper into the horse's ear.

At first the pony was quieted by the sensation of weightlessness, but then it began to twist, its front leg smacking Eddie's arm as the animal tried desperately to get some footing. Lila carefully untied the T-shirt and with both hands pushed the horse's head underwater. She tipped her face up to the stars. The horse twitched and the water splashed high. Bubbles rolled from its nostrils. Lila closed her eyes and Eddie, with his arms around its belly, tried to keep the pony steady. A few bubbles rose.

"It's almost dead," Lila whispered, loosening her hand and testing the water above the horse's face. The body slackened. She moved away, dipped her head under the sea, and put a hand to her wet hair.

Eddie let the horse go. It sank down a little, the tide moved it. Blood from the cut leg swirled thick and greasy around him. Lila was waiting in the tall swamp grass. Her features were hazy. She seemed somehow taller and Eddie felt almost afraid. But he recognized then the familiar cadence of her breath above the movement of the water and the birds' voices.

Ahead, a slow green light nudged against the shore. He walked toward it and leaned down. Lila's hand caught his. "They're worms," she said, poking one with a dry blade of grass. "And they can crawl under your skin."

···

The next day Eddie shot baskets on the cement court in front of the island school. From each point he shot a couple, then moved just a half step, paralleled his hands, flipped his wrist, and tossed the old leather ball. He was barefoot and each jump scratched his feet. They were not as tender as they had been the first shoeless days of summer, but not as rawhide hard as his mother's—pebbles stuck as he bounced.

With each shot he pictured a miniature of himself and the court, then him shooting the ball. He imagined that small version with a still smaller one, court and boy, then another tiny set, until there seemed to be a point like the speck of dust one sees in beams of light.

Lila pedaled her bike up, an outdated thing with a red banana seat, plastic ribbons whipping out from the handles and colored straws on the spokes. It was a funny kind of a bike, one he'd have made fun of in Tennessee. "Hey," Lila yelled to him.

"Where are you going?" Eddie asked, holding the ball under one arm.

"Down the beach road," she said.

He bounced the ball in a slow rhythm and listened to it thud on the asphalt.

"I wanted to tell you not to say anything," she said.

"Don't worry about that, Lila," he said.

She turned her face to the sun. He remembered her as she had been last night: first wild on the pony and then thin on shore, deflated like a wet animal.

Lila held her hand up to shield her eyes from the everywhere light. "I'll meet you after dark at the docks, okay?"

He nodded and watched her turn, pushing down hard with her tennis shoes on the fluorescent pedals.

FOUR

BLOW SMOKE

Birdflower flipped burgers at the Trolley. His long braid moved on the back of his T-shirt over Allen Ginsberg's nose, then across a bespectacled eye. Lila tacked another order above the grill and then jumped onto the kitchen counter, crossing her legs Indian-style. "Got any weed?" she asked.

Birdflower looked up. "Maybe," he said, putting down sesame-seed bun halves on the black grill.

"I see you puffing out by the dumpsters. You shoo away the cats and lean against the backside."

"What's it to you?" he said, squinting at Lila.

She played with a long strand of hair at the back of her neck. "I could tell, you know."

Birdflower pressed his spatula on the frying burgers; grease oozed up through the silver in a pattern like dog bones.

Lila's white leather sandal clicked against the bread warmer. "You never tell me anything," she said.

The owner rounded the grill. Lila hopped down with a thud onto the linoleum. "The health inspector would go crazy if he saw you sitting up there," he said.

"With longing," she said, her shorts seesawing as she walked over to the ice cream cooler.

"I need two sundaes," the owner continued. "And stop tormenting Birdflower."

Lila made a face as she bent half her body into the icy whiteness of the cooler. Waist up, she was a ghost swirling in fog. She set two scoops of vanilla, like tiny planets, into paper bowls, and added chocolate sauce from a can so sticky she had to pull hard to get it from the wooden shelf.

She leaned way over, feeling the strings of her cutoffs tickling the backs of her legs, and looked to see if Birdflower was watching. He stared straight at the grill. Lila reached into a jar with two fingers and arranged cherries on the ice cream. She pushed the sundaes through the space on the counter and rang the ladybug bell. Over the fan and grease sizzle of the friers, Lila said, "I don't need your stuff anyway."

Birdflower turned toward her and slouched back against the grill. "That's good," he said. " 'Cause you ain't gettin' any."

Lila looked at his eyes. They were set back and shriveled underneath and at the corners like old peaches. His face was similar to her father's, though her father wore his hair in a short brush cut, and his scalp was always freckled with red spots of peeling sunburn from days on the boat. There was something weathered but not settled about Birdflower, Lila thought, something like the see-through dome her aunt sent from Florida, with its tiny plastic palm trees and girls sitting cross-legged on the beach. Sand filtered in the air like visible atoms when it was shaken. As it slowed, the flat background of boats and MIAMI written in tiny oranges showed against blue sky. Birdflower's face was settled like that—you knew once it had been moving, completely shaken.

Lila watched him turn back toward the grill—faint smoke blew off the friers like the early mist leaving the marsh—his jeans bowed so low on his hips that she could see the small shadowed crack of his rear. "I know where it comes right up on the beach in bales like hay," she said.

"You're too young for that stuff," he said.

"Why do you like it?" Lila said. "Your eyes creeped-up all day."

"None of your business."

The milk shake machine and fans took over like rising night noises. With her finger, Lila drew slowly around his head, then shoulders. Traced the line where his body met the kitchen. "Old burnout," she mumbled, sticking her jaw out as if spitting in the wind.

After work, Birdflower pitched his sweatshirt onto the passenger seat while watching Lila take her break. She ate onion rings at the picnic table on the porch, listlessly looking down into the place mat scene of sailboats on a blue bay—wind like cursive drills across the sky.

He got in, drove the rattling van way up the island highway, and eased into a shallow shoulder of soft sand. No one ever believed him when he explained about his name. They all thought it was given by a guru or a favorite bedmate in a commune—but it had been his mother who called him that. As a kid he had memorized and listed the names of birds and flowers. He remembered chanting them before bed, Yellowthroat, House Finch, Lily, Killdeer, Bluebells, Bunting, Warbler, Winter Wren, Larkspur, Magpie, Murre.

The glove compartment flapped down, he shuffled maps, grabbed the plastic bag, slammed the door, and walked the path, surrounded by waving sea oats. The sun was eye level. He climbed the lifeguard platform, sat, and crossed his feet high on one side. The last light was soft on the water, its motion like tiny tame waves against the side of a bathtub. Birdflower pulled out his pipe shaped like a totem pole. He placed a pinch of weed into the bowl and lit it. He breathed the sweet smoke in, and in an easy way let it go.

Birdflower's shoulders opened, his eyes narrowed and fogged so the sea was a thin line with frayed edges. Ashes fell and rode on his curving chest hairs. Birds pattered by the water's edge; the tap-tap of their frail feet and the ocean pull on pebbles cleared his mind.

He thought of the party he'd gone to with his girlfriend the summer before he came to Ocracoke. Libby knew the people whose house it was and they were supposed to go together. But that afternoon, when he'd admitted he didn't have his half of the rent, she accused him of loafing. He'd walked to the door, said a string of things he later regretted, and left. He'd wanted to find her that night to apologize, and he'd gone into the big house filled with people and searched all the rooms on the first level. On the second-floor landing he'd seen a girl who posed at the art school and he asked her if she'd seen Libby. "She was in bad shape," the girl said, and pointed upstairs. The first bedroom he'd looked in was empty, but the next door was barred by a liquor bottle. Inside, blue from a shaded lamp illuminated Libby's nude body and a man sleeping near her. By the next week he was on the island, working at the Trolley.

Above the beach the stars winked. He lit a cigarette. Sparks scattered from the tip, and he turned his hand so the wind off the water would not interfere.

. . .

Lila sat on a stool, ate a school of pizza-flavored fish, and watched "I Love Lucy" on the black and white TV over the bar. Intermittently she wrote in her diary, brief scratchy things, pencil to her lips: today about Eddie and the pony. Lila said to the bartender, "Play a Billy Joel tape," and as it came on she mouthed the words to "Only the Good Die Young." Last summer, she'd been too young for restaurant work. So her mother, who was sick of her hanging around the house complaining about everything, had forced her to slave as a maid. She remembered dancing around the rooms, kicking into the bathrooms, and throwing herself on the beds, smoking cigarettes and watching soaps. "All My Children" as she lugged the bags of towels to the stairs. "Days of Our Lives" as she traveled from room to room making beds. "As the World Turns" when she placed new pink soaps by the tub, and "One Life to Live" as she did mirrors, the glass always clearing to her face in a cloud of cigarette smoke.

"Can I have another Coke," Lila said. "With two cherries this time."

The bartender shook his blond head. "Your teeth will rot right out of your mouth."

Lila thought she heard Birdflower's voice outside the bar. She'd been waiting for an hour. He always came to the bar when his day shift was finished. Her plan was to approach him for a joint. She figured she'd have a better chance of him saying yes in front of his friends. They might even ask her to sit with them. They'd tell drug stories, like the few Birdflower had on those first slow kitchen afternoons. What she liked to hear best were the stories of him getting stoned and feeling like a genius, like he knew with perfect clarity how everything connected.

She pretended not to see him come through the door with David and Michael, the guys who ran the tourist sailboat, and head for the corner table. In a minute, a waitress brought mugs and a pitcher of beer.

David put his bare feet up on the table and told Birdflower

about a tourist they took out on the boat. "One of these divorcees," he said. "Gold jewelry. Silk tank top. She pulled a stick of butter from her cooler."

"Peeled the foil off the tip," Michael added, and showed with his fingers. Birdflower smiled. "Then she rubbed it on her nipples. They were the size of half-dollars."

"Needless to say," David said, "we took her out a little farther than usual."

All three laughed as Michael tipped the pitcher to fill the mugs.

Birdflower said, "Some good weed's coming up from Florida around the end of the month."

"Yeah," David said. "That last batch wasn't worth shit."

"You know Emily?" Birdflower said.

"Of course we know Emily." Michael smiled, thinned his lips over his teeth.

"Can she come along fishing next weekend?"

"That would be up to you," David said. "Long as that islander isn't with her."

Lila rehearsed what she would say, drank the rest of her Coke, and headed back to their table.

"Got one doobie?" she said, firmly like drug addicts she'd seen on TV.

Birdflower put his head down. "Not for you."

"You think I'm a baby." Lila raised her voice. "You think you're great," she said. "All your long hair and stupid stories."

"What do you want?" Birdflower said.

She placed a stray hand on her hip. "Weed," she said.

"Get out of here, Lila," the bartender yelled.

Birdflower rocked back on his chair. "Go play," he said.

She ran out with her hands over her face. He saw the backs of her tan legs—thin and spindly as a colt's. "If I were a couple years younger." Birdflower turned back toward the table. "She'd be trouble."

· · ·

With a full moon behind the cedars, Lila walked along the sand street and saw the family graveyards to one side, old stones and new ones in plots no bigger than a modest front yard. She touched the white fence surrounding her family's plot. "I know things," she said out loud.

She'd been off the island a dozen times, to Hatteras, Nags Head, once on a class trip to Washington, D.C., which was lush, not the weathered beige of everything on the island. All the way up the coast, rows of tobacco plants spread out as straight as lines on paper. Every few miles, there was a trailer or shack, and women in pastel-flowered housedresses sitting in lawn chairs, flesh jiggling on their upper arms. It went on forever. Lila always imagined them driving off the island, riding underwater, seeing big fish, the car's headlights shining on pink seaweed and purple coral. Washington was like another planet, with those marble buildings as straight and white as space stations and the artifacts in them, carefully chosen and numbered. Lila thought if the world ended it wouldn't matter, because like the flood in the Bible, there would be at least two of everything left. Best of all, she liked the long dark hallway of tall and stately first ladies. Everyone in evening gowns of sequins, taffeta, or silk. The young ones were her favorites, because she could see herself among them, a tanless woman, mannequin-thin, with a built-in sophistication. On the way home, she'd fallen asleep against the back seat and dreamed of ladies, swirling elegantly, moving their slender arms and necks slowly in time with the waltz. There was one in a green dress—tiny metallic-looking beads sewn close together like scales—who was dancing with Lila, holding her in her arms, her simple movements telling Lila everything. But when Lila looked up, it was into gluey fish eyes and the woman was a slippery sea trout with its gills winged out frantically.

Something stirred in the low branches over the graveyard. Lila shivered. She saw her grandmother's gravestone and the row of plastic violets she put there herself in April. "There's a disease called Island Fever," her grandmother once said as she and Lila walked along the beach, bending occasionally to pick up striped scallop shells. "I read once how cows get loose and run into the ocean." Lila had seen a few of the wild ponies knee-deep, looking out over the water, but they always seemed to come back. She dragged her toe along the packed sand road and imagined whole herds of cows swimming underwater, galloping in slow motion over starfish and sand dollars, their moos bubbling up to the surface.

"Birdflower," she said, then sang it in different melodies and at various speeds all the way to her house. She said it so many times it lost all meaning and became only sounds. The bedroom door banged behind her. Lila flopped across her flowered bedspread. With a little of his weed she would forget everything: the ugly trailers by the coast guard station, the raggedy string of T-shirt shacks, and the pony, that queasy bone that had poked her underwater. *Yes.* With his pot she would float up, look down on all this, and laugh.

In the morning, Lila watched Birdflower hosing off with the spigot in back of the Trolley Stop. He undid his hair, tips hanging nearly to his waist. He wet it, then sprayed water down his pants and under his armpits, and then sat in the sun and braided his hair back up.

Lila poured six large Cokes into striped cups, the last overflowing.

"Quit your dreaming," the owner shouted. "And get those up here."

Lila stuck out her tongue and rolled her eyes.

Dripping, Birdflower came in and reached for the mayo and ketchup tubs in the refrigerator.

Lila counted out loud all the jars of green pickles shelved above her. "A lifetime supply," she said, brushing Birdflower and stepping around the puddle by his feet.

He tipped his chin. "Why did you do that yesterday?" he said. "What's the big deal?"

The grill began to sizzle. It smelled like grease. Birdflower scraped it with a spatula.

"All I want is some of your stuff," she said flatly.

Birdflower looked at the faint circles like crescent moons under her eyes.

"And back here we could talk," Lila said, pointing to the dumpsters. "During breaks we could smoke out there."

Birdflower held out his hand. "I don't know anything," he said.

The lights blinked. "Goddamnit!" the owner said from the front. "Those underwater lines aren't worth crap." Everything went dead. The fans slowly wound down and the grill crackled lightly. "Break," the owner said, shaking his head.

Lila followed Birdflower behind the dumpster. The sky was ultravox blue. Cats weaved around their feet and dived to the weeds from the top edge of the dumpster. He pulled a joint out of his T-shirt pocket, lit it, and breathed in. "First puff of the day," he said, eyes closing from the morning glare.

"Just one drag," Lila said. She reached and picked up a scrawny cat; its back legs hung loose under her arm.

"You'll burn yourself," Birdflower said.

Lila dropped the cat. "Blow smoke in my mouth then."

He breathed in, his hand held backward and his lips tight together. Birdflower motioned with his head for her to come closer. Lila made her mouth a slack, choirboy oval.

Birdflower put his lips inches away and blew blue-gray smoke into her mouth. She held it, forced it down, and pictured it spreading in her lungs like smoke in a white room. "Again," she said. He took a drag, leaned closer this time so their lips just barely did not touch. Lila closed her eyes. "All I want to know is how far you have to go before you can come back." Birdflower pulled back and listened for the sound of water moving out on the point. When he passed her the joint, their fingers touched.

The owner yelled, "Electricity's on."

FIVE

FISH MARKET

B *efore noon* on Sunday, Emily left the house and the outer arc of dappling leaf light and headed toward town to meet Eddie. She had on khaki shorts, washed soft as skin, and a blouse that gathered around the neck with a green ribbon. Her sunglasses hid the bluish bruise around her left eye and reached over half of one of the larger scabs on her forehead.

Emily's street was the only complete sand one; all the rest that crisscrossed over the island were either gravel or cement. And the sloppy roads on the soundside were often marked with boards. In the winter the population dwindled to less than six hundred, but

now there were two thousand or more, counting tourists and summer residents. The island itself was shaped like a thermometer.
The Texaco, Trolley, and Paolo's were along the fourteen miles of
highway that led to Silver Lake. The town horseshoed around that
inlet. On the northwest tip was the coast guard station, then the
tourist docks, post office, community store, and the old Victorian
houses. These were inhabited by captains' widows who, some people said, still smoked opium as they had earlier while waiting for
their husbands to return from the sea. A dozen long docks radi-
ated into Silver Lake, and the commercial fishing boats and
shrimpers docked there alongside locals' rowboats and tourist sailboats. On the northernmost point stood the lighthouse, and near
it a storybook Pentecostal church. Emily had been there once, and
she remembered the snapdragons in milk glass vases on the altar.

Her sandals flipped sand against the back of her bare legs, and
she rested for a moment on the gate of one of the small family
cemeteries. The stones were granite, most with simple crosses,
names, and dates. Above her, a sparrow landed on a low cedar
branch. She remembered her father and how in sermons he would
use her and her sister Sarah as examples of naturally sinful children, telling things to the whole congregation—never smiling or
looking down to where his family sat in the front pew.

It was Easter sunrise she liked to think about in detail. There
was always a huge cross twisted with forsythia and braced with
gold cord. The altar guild ladies brought lilies in their cars. The
big trumpet blossoms pressed against the glass. Around five-thirty
the light diffused. A piano arrived in the back of a pickup truck.
Her father's cape arched out from his shoulders. Fifty or so mem-
bers sat in folding chairs and there were another twenty like Emily
and her mother in cars. The organist banged out the Alleluia and
it was then that she always felt herself dissolving. Only the sight of
her father, his blond hair backlit by the sun, anchored her.

Emily came out of the tunneled trees and crossed the main

street to the post office. She was a few minutes early, so she sat down on the sidewalk curb and squinted across the parking lot.

Eddie had gone at low tide to clam. She'd offered to help but he'd refused, saying they would meet later near the market to pick out a fish for dinner. He had insisted on coming, she knew, because he loved the mackerel and bluefish lined on ice, the delicate filleting knives and the loose scales that stuck to everything.

Though he'd asked several times, she still hadn't told him why John Berry had thrown the bottle. She figured he understood, but he seemed to want her to say something about her lovers and Emily was unsure if she could.

She felt a damp hand grab the back of her neck, and Eddie sat down, slung the net bag of clams between his legs, and laid the rake next to him.

"You got all those by yourself?" Emily said.

"Yeah. Let's go get the fish." He seemed oddly anxious.

Emily heard a rustle behind her and turned to see the branches of a bush near the P.O. shake. Under the white blossoms and leaves were a girl's bare legs in a pair of wet tennis shoes.

"Who's that?" Emily asked.

"Lila," he said. "She wanted to see you up close."

Lila walked a step behind Emily and Eddie across the gravel parking lot, up the wooden stairs, and into the small room. There was hardly enough space for the three of them to stand in front of the rows of fish on ice. The place was deserted and Lila felt a little creepy under the silent surveillance of so many dead eyes.

Eddie stood a few yards away and kicked at a muddy box near the far wall. Lila fingered the fish, grabbed the tails, and twisted them, checking for firmness with her index finger. She could tell from the way Emily stayed near the door and folded her arms heavily in front of her that she didn't like the headless fish, or even the shimmering whole ones.

Lila stared at her and Emily seemed to sense it; she straightened her shoulders, tipped up her chin, and let her eyes become distant. A few months ago Lila had seen Emily shopping at the community store, barefoot and in tattered jeans; she bought only four things—a gallon of red wine, a tall white candle, bath bubbles, and some condoms.

Emily read the cardboard price list and commented on how shrimp were particularly cheap this week. "I've heard you were the fastest header on the island," she said to Lila.

"I didn't know that," Eddie said.

Lila could tell by the eager tone in his voice that this impressed him.

She blushed; it was a fact she'd always been proud of, but picturing herself among the other island women, hair up, sitting on her milking stool, and twisting handfuls of shrimp heads off until her fingers were raw, seemed embarrassing to her now.

"Pruitt's usually in the back," Lila said, and she walked past Emily out the screen door and around to where he was slicing a shark into steaks. The sun was hot. Emily had probably meant to be flattering, but Lila felt uncomfortable because she couldn't be sure. Pruitt's white apron was bloody, and there were even specks of blood in his hair. She watched him cut through the spine, then into the softer muscle of the fish. "You got customers," Lila told him.

"First ones," Pruitt said. "Thought I might get to sit around all day till my dad started me on this."

He motioned to the sprawl of silver skin and wet bones. She watched the white shrimper *Last Chance* sway in the water near the market. While he hosed off his hands, she counted the shark heads in a brown bag, then pressed a finger into a puddle of blood on the filleting board. Lila smelled the blood and then wiped it off on the wood boards. She remembered how her grandmother had told her that drinking the blood of animals passed their powers on to you. She watched Pruitt dry his hands on some newspaper. He was her age, but because he was so silent and lanky, Lila thought of him as younger.

She followed him through the maze of packing coolers in the back way. "Pruitt was gutting a shark in the back," Lila said. She paused to see if they would grimace or cringe. Emily concentrated on the fish, pretending not to hear, but Eddie scowled at her and averted his eyes, and Lila felt guilty for trying to shock them.

Emily pointed, "How about that one?"

Pruitt picked the trout up, weighed it, and threw it on the butcher block. He asked if she wanted it cleaned. Emily shook her head. He slid the trout into a clear bag, so its face pressed against the plastic.

Emily paid, and there was something in the gentle way she took the bag with both hands that gave Lila the feeling she wasn't going to cook the trout at all.

JULY

In early July the ferry at dusk is never crowded. Most crossers stay in the sleepy comfort of their cars listening to the last hints of Norfolk radio and letting the lurch of the boat lull them. Really it's only lovers on long weekends that go out into the windy confusion to lean against the bow's rail. They listen to the rigging clang and the crack and pull of the flags and watch water heave up in the wake of the ferry. Their sweatshirts puff up like blowfish. Against the darkening foreground they see the tipped wingspans and shiny beaks of the hundreds of gulls that swoop and circle, following the boat in hopes of handfuls of white bread or crackers. Lovers in July look ahead to the lights of the island. Somehow only they know that the power of air is all and they must come wordless into the sing of wind and water.

SIX

DEEP SEA FISHING

Emily *pulled* her T-shirt off in one smooth movement, her hair fell back to her shoulders, her bikini-top triangles of rose macramé shook slightly, and the shells tied to the back strings tinkled like wind chimes. The white shirt she held blew out like a flag as the cruiser bumped over the water. Birdflower's clean brown hair was gathered in a ponytail and tucked into a pale lavender T-shirt with maroon mermaids singing on the front. She watched his lips move, but because of the boat's engine, she couldn't make out the words.

They were sitting on cushions along the far wall of the boat, watching the island melt to water. Before them were the fishing chairs, bolted swivel seats. In the front, Michael steered behind the splattered Plexiglas window of the cabin. Near him, David tipped a beer to his lips; the can touched the rim of his baseball cap. She saw how Birdflower looked at the brass bead held by a leather string around her neck and the smooth sheen of her hair. His eyes lingered on the swell of her breasts. Water spray dotted their faces. He leaned over and cupped a hand to her ear. "I'll catch you something," he said.

Emily looked ahead of the boat and imagined the Gulf Stream. "Like the ocean has a light blue racing stripe," Birdflower had said. She thought it was like a sunbeam, coming up from Florida and the Gulf of Mexico, illuminating fish in the sea's dark room.

The last time she'd been fishing was with Eddie, when he was ten, at sunset; she remembered how excited he'd been, casting, wading out barefoot in his rolled-up jeans. She had sat in a lawn chair on the sand and watched his tanned back moving in the surf. Now he wouldn't want to fish. He was busy with Lila.

Birdflower got a beer from the cooler near the bait bundles and the longer cooler for fish. The beer popped, fizzed; he took a sip and handed it to Emily. Michael steered with one hand and pointed. "There's the Gulf," he said. He wore the thick fisherman sunglasses that wrapped around his face, protecting even his peripheral vision from the sun. The engine kicked and sputtered and the boat made a lazy arc in the water.

Birdflower moved to help with the anchor. Michael winked at Emily. "You just sit there and look pretty," he said.

She smiled. She liked being the only woman among men. It set the curves of her body off like the stems of flowers against a hard wall. The fishing rods bent like willows.

Birdflower stood near her and slipped a hand to her waist. He had on bright surfing pants that Emily thought were too young for him. The stiff, starched cotton brushed against her thigh.

Birdflower undid the squid pieces packed in butcher paper.

They were purple with white spots and shaped like broccoli stems. He baited her hook, his hands moving as if each finger had a small brain at the tip. Once last season she crept behind the sand dunes. It was strange: water up to Birdflower's thighs, an old onion sack filled with clams over his shoulder. He was mindless, looking up often into the sun, blinking when it flashed in his eyes. The warm water must have aroused him because she saw the way he fiddled with his bathing suit, how he eventually dropped the rake and held himself in both hands. She remembered the angles: flat water to the horizon, thick strip of sky, and his body heaving back in diagonal to them.

Birdflower leaned against the side of the boat. "I saw you yesterday on the beach road," he said.

"Yeah, I've been around."

Birdflower kicked one sneaker against the toe of the other. "That's what I've heard."

Emily was surprised that he would say that. "Why can't I do what I want?" she said.

Birdflower looked out over the water. "Women like you will always have trouble in this world," he said.

David suddenly gave a banshee cry and did a cannonball off the side of the boat. Michael dove straight and Emily saw him glide for a moment underwater. When he rose, he asked if they were coming in.

Birdflower looked at Emily. "Go ahead," she said. "I'll watch."

He dropped himself over backwards like a scuba diver. Emily stood and put a knee over the edge as if she was riding sidesaddle.

David swam around the hull, checking for chipped paint or soft spots in the wood. Birdflower kept his feet up and paddled his hands. The men in the water looked similar as otters and their wet hair and shoulders gleamed. She imagined huge schools of fish extending beneath them. She imagined the prickle of scales as the fish undulated. Sometimes she would find herself thinking of fish and feel a muscle, a *swim* come over her. Emily loved whales because of the way they moved, quietly as clouds. She still remembered how she and Eddie had played in the inlet. Underneath they swam together and apart as whales do, circling, somersaulting; they seemed much bigger than themselves in the dark water. She was also fascinated with the goosefish. She'd talked one morning to a shaken-looking man from Manteo. He had been fishing on the point and claimed to have seen a goosefish, tiny teeth like ivory nails, clamp down and pull a low-flying piper under the surface. Lately she'd been watching the scrawled filefish that lolled in Pamlico Sound. They were gluey white, with the small eyes of a scholar, and each had a different pattern of shapes, like some exotic language, etched over its skin.

Emily left the boat's edge, leaned back in her chair and closed her eyes. She always felt as if she were swimming in a maze of fish, patterns over her body of light and water.

Later in the afternoon, Emily watched Birdflower on deck. A few hairs blew out of his braid and floated free from his head. Neither of them had even had a nibble all day, but earlier, at noon, David had caught a small dolphin that had flapped on deck—its blue skin stretched thin like a balloon. The small eyes and tender pale belly reminded Emily of a baby and she'd convinced them to throw him back.

The beer made her head light. She saw Birdflower watching the bones in her neck and shoulders. She felt tugs from her line now and then, but no real tension.

"Look," David said.

Emily flipped her head to the dolphin threading in and out of water.

Birdflower jerked back. "I got something." He pushed his feet into the floor, clamping down on the pole, and pulled his weight back.

The fish, a thin muscle, flipped out of the sea. "It's a sword," Michael said.

The pole jerked toward the water. Birdflower leaned back. Emily watched his knuckles whiten. She stood and moved her hand to his shoulder. As she was trying to follow the fin, she saw the image of John Berry over the water. She knew he was there to let her know he thought Birdflower was an insubstantial kind of man and that it was weak for her to start up with him. His face was stern like the pirates from whom he'd descended. Emily would forget the islanders were kin to Blackbeard, but then on Friday nights they'd come out to Paolo's, and when a fast song clicked and fell in the jukebox, they'd do a crazy shuffle step—jeans rolled to their knees, smelling like fish and sun—they swung their long-haired girlfriends.

The fish buckled above water. Her hair blew back hard, and she had to bring her head forward to steady herself. If he'd been able to, she knew John Berry would have accused her of letting him think nothing was wrong, of making him look like a lovesick fool. She wanted to tell him that in her own way she had felt for him. There were things, triggers, his boyish hand movements, curls like the fine fur of pheasants on the back of his neck, and sometimes with him there had been an abandon.

The sword's top fin skimmed the water. "Talk to me," Birdflower said.

Emily felt hungry and a little dizzy, and again when she looked out over the water, she saw John Berry and her hands tightened on Birdflower's shoulders. It seemed to her it was him, snagged and straining on the end of the line. "Think of it like a man," she said into his ear.

Michael gave her a puzzled look. "What are you doing?"

"Let her go," Birdflower said.

The swordfish was twenty yards away, the line tight as a guitar string. Emily watched it buck at the surface. "He's calling you names," Emily whispered.

Birdflower grimaced and held on. She tightened her grip on his arm and felt tension through his skin. There was a sudden tug. Birdflower lost his grip and the line reeled out.

"A breakaway," David said. "Pull back."

Birdflower did, but the line slackened and blew.

Everyone was quiet and the water too seemed calm. The sudden stillness felt eerie to Emily and she walked over to the edge to look for a flicker or a slash of fin. If he caught the fish, she knew they'd string it up and take pictures, like those at the restaurant behind the cash register, photos of grinning men with beers held high to the camera. There were hundreds of these, some overlapping so only the fish showed, the pictures forming a school of minnows swimming off the restaurant wall.

The line went taut again and Birdflower pulled his body back, then caught the slack and wound in. This went on till Emily heard the fish bump the side of the boat. The net clapped water, and as they raised it, Emily saw the fish wrapped in rope. On deck, it hissed and flipped. Birdflower beamed over the sword. She reached to the back fin, chrome-green and familiar, ridges fanning out like a wet feather.

The swordfish steaks cooked in the black skillet, turning from a transparent pink marble to firm white. They swam in butter, mushrooms, and scallion bits. "Cajun style," Birdflower said, standing over the stove. He took a sip from his wine, then set it down. "It's exciting. Life on the end of your line."

"My heart went thump, thump, thump," Emily said.

She watched from her chair at a yellow table in his one-room cottage, an unmade bed in the far corner. On the wall, photos of suns over water. And leaning against the far wall, his guitar, a ukulele, and a big Western twelve-string.

"How old's your boy?" Birdflower asked, the fish crackling behind him.

"Sixteen."

Birdflower shook his head. "You with a kid that old?"

"I don't see what's so strange about it. Some women have babies at twelve," Emily said.

"White trash women." Birdflower grinned.

"It's more than some have to show for themselves," Emily said.

"I just don't think of you as a mother."

She pointed to the photos. "Which ones are which?"

"The blood-orange suns, the ones like coals, are the sunsets. The other ones are mornings."

Emily stared at the dawn suns, which were grayer and seemed to have a kind of music in them; flute, guitar.

He set down seashore-pattern plates bordered with tiny umbrellas and beach balls. "Former tenants," he said.

Emily gazed to the bongs, rolling papers, and pipes scattered among his things. "You smoke a lot, don't you?"

"Yeah," he said. "But not like you might think."

She watched him lever up the fish and peek underneath.

For months bodies had blurred in her mind. Lips, puffs of underarm hair, the swell and curve of a fleshy calf. John Berry had become familiar, like a brother it seemed; he held her in the nights. But the thought of him fell away each time she strayed. He became a blind spot with the whoosh of her clothes landing on the floor. With strangers there were ten minutes of unornamented reality. A kind of mainline black rush of being alive in the most obvious, necessary way. Her whole life was lived for these: cheek to the hollow space between back and shoulder, arm resting in arm, legs wrinkled together.

With the spatula, Birdflower put a sword steak onto her plate and then poured butter and squares of onions over it. It smelled intoxicating. The gallon of wine swayed slightly as he raised it between them. Emily felt her hand cupped around a wineglass, the other resting on her thigh, and her back against the metal of the chair. She settled into herself and lifted her glass for more.

SEVEN

MTV

*S*nowflakes *and* stars, no color really, just shapes suggesting silver or white made by the pressure of his fingertips on his eyes. Lila was stretched out next to him. Her head rested on the tab of a huge Miller beer—and her arms and legs sprawled over the towel's edge. "Never?" he said pressing harder.

"You know I've heard of 'em. The channel we get from Nags Head just has drag racing and reruns. Every time I turn it on, those cars that look like water bugs are rounding the track."

"Too bad," Eddie said, fingering the swimsuit his mother had bought him: long shorts, with a drawstring waist and bright shapes floating in canary yellow. He remembered his favorite video: Sting messing up a ballroom, then following a blonde into a Rolls-Royce.

"What's so great about them?" Lila asked.

"They're like movies," he said, "but better, the best part of movies, when stuff is happening and there's music."

"I like listening to music," Lila said, her eyes closed. Tiny beads of sweat gathered on her upper lip and brow. "What's so great about getting a few more channels?"

"MTV is not a TV channel," Eddie said.

"You turn it on the dial, don't you? It's little color and light particles in the air like all the others."

"I can't explain it." He shook his head, leaned back on his palm tree–patterned towel, and put his sunglasses back on. "It's beyond words." Eddie saw a thin and unshaven rock star, diamond stud in one ear, singing to her. "They're like dreams," he said.

"Not any I've had," Lila said and turned her head.

"Take my word for it."

"Does your mother?"

"What does that have to do with anything?"

"If they're all that great, I'd bet she'd like them," Lila said. She started talking about his mom the way she always did, as though she were some sort of magical person, different from everyone else on the island.

Eddie half listened; he looked down to the public beach where kids in the surf caught tame waves as far up the sand as their father's feet. Sometimes in Tennessee—the ground covered with snow, his dog Sebastian sending wet puffs up in front of him, the ice-covered trees tingling like angels—Eddie would wonder about Ocracoke and the island winters there. He'd daydream about high waves drenching his mother's house, the water sitting for days till it froze and encased things: the red bathroom trash can with the British hunters on it; the bag of oranges near the refrigerator; his mother's soft leather sandals with the darker sunken spot for each toe. But rising water wasn't really what he worried about. He thought mostly of her and how restless she would be during the winter rainstorms. He wondered if she missed him. It bothered Eddie that she never asked to see him in the winters. He wondered if she drank too much, if she was careful in the ocean, and what the men she was with were like.

Eddie interrupted Lila and asked her what it was like on the island in the winter.

"You never listen to me," she said.

"Yeah, I do."

"You act like I'm some kind of ape or something," Lila said.

Eddie thought of her being a delicate baby ape. Like the tiny monkeys in lace dresses he'd seen on talk shows.

"Everything closes," Lila said, "and we all sit around and stare at each other."

Gulls were edging closer. With heads cocked they eyed the sweaty Coke cans and bag of chips.

"I'm sorry," Eddie said. He waited for her to answer. "Want to come to my house tonight? I got some beers. And my mother won't be back until late—she's deep-sea fishing."

"Sure," Lila said lazily. "I got nothing better to do." As if she just thought of it, Lila leaned up and moved her lips close to his ear. "I heard they found that pony."

Eddie said, "No one knows . . ."

"Just you and me," Lila said, lying back down. They were quiet a moment. "If you want, we could go to the lighthouse after."

"Really?"

"My father helped paint it last year and he still has keys."

"But let's drink the beers first at my house."

"Okay."

She got up quickly and went to the water. He followed, thinking of it like a movie: high steps through the waves, then in slow motion diving into the sea.

"The waves come in sevens," Lila said. She breaststroked toward his open hand. Eddie pulled her to his lap where she floated light as balsa wood above his knees. She noticed his hair curled up around his face and how the longer pieces on the back of his neck waved. "Do you ever tell lies?" she said.

"No," he said, looking way off to the blurry horizon. But swift as a good pin, he thought of the time he was caught shoplifting albums under his shirt, and how the cellophane had stuck to his chest. Also the fibs he'd told this summer, mostly to tourist girls, that he played tight end at college, had been an extra in a movie.

"I do, all the time," she said.

"Why?" Eddie said. He held her as gently as possible. Cigarette-thin fish turned together toward them, their pale underwater legs an obstacle, then the school formed like geese and headed back to shore.

"Nearly everything I say is a lie," Lila said, her arms in a loose ribbon around Eddie's neck. "I just start going and I see whatever I'm talking about like usual. But then it has on a new dress, or a green ring, or maybe the words somebody said are funnier."

"Lying's for kids," Eddie said.

Lila said, "Your mother lies."

"She never lied to me," Eddie said, seeing thousands of his mother's lies coming out from her mouth in written words as if she was a sword swallower pulling out a hundred swords.

Lila snuggled her head into Eddie's neck. He liked the easy motion of the waves breaking behind them. His mother still had a few bruises the color of bird eggs and one heart-shaped scab on her temple. He put his cheek to Lila's wet hair. "Meet me at the dock tonight. Then we'll go to my house."

"Then to the lighthouse," Lila said. She slipped her arm down around his waist and they floated, pulled by the ocean but anchored underwater by Eddie's toes sunk into liquid sand.

· · ·

Eddie rode his skateboard into the few funnels of street lamp light and through the dark connecting spaces of night. He pumped fast in jeans, black high-tops, and a BOBCAT sweatshirt. He rolled off the asphalt and onto the cement walk. At the first dock, Lila sat swaying her feet above the water. Around her the lit cabins of boats shined like lanterns. He watched her in the picture of sailboats, dark sky, and water.

Island boys cruised by in a jeep; he heard empty beer cans rattling between their legs and saw a green-tattooed arm and cigarettes in a shirt rolled over a muscular bicep.

He watched Lila. He liked how she lay on her stomach in the sun with her little fists curved under her hip bones. She said things that were hard to forget, that swung round in him like a pebble in a hubcap.

Eddie picked up his board and walked under the big, dark sky. He thought of the time when he was thirteen in the church with a girl who reminded him of Lila. They found the open side door of the local Methodist church and lay toe to toe in the center pew, the long stained glass windows deep with royal blues, ocean greens, and burgundy. It was the girl who had suggested that they strip down to underwear and lie still, catching holy light through glass figures of Jesus, John the Baptist, Moses, and Mary. His head rested on his jeans. Eddie remembered her body and his in a hazy aura and how he tried to make out her breasts and then the altar up ahead, just one hanging candle showing deep tones in the velvet fairlane.

"You're late," Lila yelled up from the dock. He heard a cling-clang crawling sound and saw a pail of crabs. In her hands was the white cord she teased them with. Over the edge he saw crabs clawing on a barnacled dock post. The dock smelled of charcoal, a lazy banjo tune tinkled from a sailboat anchored in the inlet, and a cluster of tourists in lawn chairs were settled near their rocking boats. They drank gin from mismatched glasses and talked sleepily among themselves. "I almost got one," Lila said, hand over long-fingered hand, pulling the string up. "It's a baby," she said. She wriggled the line and let it drop.

"Ready?" Eddie said. The banjo notes drifted over the water. The crabs crawled over each other to get out. He wanted to be home where the beers were on ice. He'd made his bed and selected a few tapes, piling all his laundry discreetly in the closet.

"I knew a boy off one of these boats," she said. "He was going to play the clarinet in a circus band. He had this tune he was thinking would be perfect for the elephant routine. And another one for the poodles."

"I saw a circus," Eddie said, picking up the pail and leading her away. "This lady in a sparkly bikini did tricks on a high bar. No safety net or anything. It was like she'd jump right into your lap. The program said she was afraid of city traffic." He slipped an arm around her waist. "Isn't that weird?"

"Yeah," Lila said. "It's like my father. He's out in the ocean with his pound nets every day but he can hardly swim." She matched her body to his stride. The lighthouse shone like a candle on the trees of the wild side of the island.

Eddie asked if she had the keys. Lila nodded. "I almost snagged the ones for my father's truck, too."

"That would've been great."

"Yeah," Lila said, "but he keeps them with him most of the time." She stopped and looked carefully at him. "Don't think anything is going to happen." She put her hand into his jeans pocket.

Eddie heard a crab scratch. He heard his heart like a tom-tom in his head and he felt her pulse through her fingers.

"I've had beer before," Lila said as they sat on his bed popping two of the assorted brands, some green bottles with fancy labels, a few cans, all sneaked from the restaurant. They leaned against the wall of his bedroom, light only from the tape deck. He gulped his beer, embarrassed by the purple beads his mother had strung across the doorway and pulled to one side with a shoelace. The room was paneled gray barn color with a matching twin bed and dresser wedged in and had a view of the porch chair swing moving slightly through sheer curtains.

"I drank a six once. Threw up for three days," Lila said. Her dice earrings rocked. Eddie put his hand on her knee.

The crabs they'd put on the stove earlier plopped and tangled in the big kitchen pot.

"Why?" Eddie asked, eyeing the racing magazines in piles by the bed and remembering the one smuggled *Playboy* down near the bottom.

"I was bored," Lila said. "It was at a bonfire on the beach. Everybody else was either passed out, or making out."

Eddie got a tall brown bottle. "Dark's stronger," he said, putting his hand back on her knee and thinking of the scars there, a design like fishhooks and question marks. Like an instrument in its velvet cradle, the small dark room seemed to fit them perfectly. She leaned onto his shoulder and Eddie felt little mad-scientist currents between them. As in the movies he kissed her full on the mouth, then moved an unsure hand to her. There was worry that if it came down to it, he wouldn't know what to do, he would be awkward, and the chance to make love to Lila would crackle and evaporate. His mind ran with scattered bits friends had told him and information he had gotten from other girls.

Lila whispered, "What's that noise?"

Eddie heard crabs, crabs bailing out, a quick claw over the edge and then one by one each hurling its weight over. "Water's not hot enough," he said.

"They'll get all over your house." Lila giggled. "Like little trolls."

"I like it," Eddie said, pulling her to him and trying to roll them horizontal on the sandy sheets. Crabs continued to jump like paratroopers. Lila's body felt as fragile as the swans glassblowers form. A breeze that smelled of leaves goose-pimpled his legs and blew the curtains inward. He heard drunken voices singing up the road. A man said something about warm water. "That's my mother," Eddie said and sat up.

Emily sang: "How does it *feel?*" And the man joined in, "To be on your own—"

"That's Birdflower," Lila said. "What's he doing with her?"

"How am I supposed to know? Maybe they're drunk from the boat," Eddie said. "Let's go." He got up and pulled her hand. "Come on."

"I thought you said your mother was taking a break."

"Lila, let's go." Eddie saw his mother up the road under the moon. With her skirt held up she kicked her legs.

They left with a bang of the kitchen door, running fast in the moonlight along the sand road. Eddie slowed only when he could no longer make out the words of his mother's song.

"This is the oldest operating lighthouse on the east coast," Lila said, fingers pinching her nose, putting on her tour guide voice. The key clicked in the lock and the door opened. Eddie stepped behind her into the complete roundness of the lighthouse. He looked up the spiral stairs to the latchdoor with light around the cracks, as if the sun was on the other side. Their feet made metallic sounds on the stairs. "Around three times," Lila said, taking Eddie's hand. "For luck."

He watched her climb the stairs to the light. When Lila turned, her eyes flicked red like dogs in photographs. "We would be dead if we fell," she said.

Eddie caught his breath.

"What's with you?"

"Nothing," Eddie said.

"My grandmother said one keeper fell and that he deserved it because he was drunk."

Eddie dragged a hand on the cool wall. "Did he break his legs?"

"Both legs were folded under like a doll's," Lila said and pushed the wooden door open.

They climbed into a round room with windows. Three giant bulbs in cone-shaped silver reflectors elevated in the middle spun and flashed. "Like a spaceship, I always think," Lila said as she walked to the side with the view of the Atlantic. Eddie thought of sea captains in heavy wool coats with velvet collars looking up to the light on shore. Maybe in a split second, this one captain in his boat, at the wheel near Bermuda or farther, would see Lila and him leaning against each other by the window. Eddie looked down to the jagged shoreline, rocks below thinning threads of water.

Lila broke from him. "Look at the island," she said, and walked barefoot to the other side. The view flashed of white cottages, small sailboats, a few motels, the community store, the bar, and even the beginnings of the beach—a hint of motion on the far side.

"It's like it's play from up here," she said. "I think the lighthouse keepers were really afraid of water. I think they came up here, not really looking to the water for ships in trouble, but instead standing and looking over the island trying to see their wife's tiny hands in the kitchen window drying a dinner plate."

Eddie wanted to say something. The wind keened around the lighthouse. Quickly he spidered his fingers up Lila's back and felt for the hook of her bra. It came undone easily, slackened, and fell lazily. Light pulsed on their mouths pressed like kissing fish. He and Lila kneeled together on the floor like children, then fell under the beams of strong light flashing above them and out over the sea for miles.

EIGHT

THE FOURTH

The firecracker, tossed from the cracked door of the men's room, rolled like a cigarette, then exploded.

"Get 'em out of there," John Berry said from outside to the boy's father who lay flat out, bare-bellied, on the hood of his car.

"Let the kid have some fun. It's the U.S. of A.'s birthday," he said, cocking one eye as he spoke.

John Berry shook his head. "Look," he said. He smelled barbecue and Budweiser on the man's breath. "We're not on solid ground here."

The boy in the bathroom opened the door. John Berry saw his

thin arms and hands lighting the tip of another firecracker. John Berry lunged for him, but the boy tossed the cracker, slammed the door, and laughed. The firecrackers rang and smoked near the car's front tires. "Bring me some more matches, Pop," the boy said.

"Get out of there, kid," John Berry said. He pounded on the door, then looked pleadingly at the boy's father, who gave him a lazy stare and calmly tipped a beer to his lips. "I'd bet today must have been hell for a guy like you."

John Berry stared at the father. He could see, even in the dusk, the white lines on his stomach that in the sun had been shaded by fat.

"Tell your kid to get out of there," John Berry said.

The door cracked open and he saw the boy's face. "You don't own this boat," he said. He lobbed a whole row of firecrackers past John Berry's arm and all the way to the railing. *Rat-a-tat-tat.* John Berry's neck tightened. He really didn't want to hassle the kid. He was afraid to see even a shade of that expression, the one Emily'd had before he threw the bottle—pretended innocence and then fear.

"I've got some sparklers," he said to the boy. "Would you come out for that?"

The boy didn't answer and John Berry heard his feet scuffing on the tiles as though he was shadowboxing.

John Berry turned. "Yeah," the father said. "We're driving straight through to Jersey tonight." He gestured in the air with an open hand.

John Berry shook his head and walked down the metal steps. Opening his locker, he grabbed the sparklers out of the bag that contained his beer and cigarettes. The long red and white box reminded him of last year when he'd gotten off for the Fourth and Emily and he had gone to a cookout. He remembered her bare shoulders in a sundress and how, as it darkened, her skin blurred as if she were underwater. Most of the night she sat on a low-slung wooden porch chair with a floral cushion, talking to Tom's wife, and he'd sat across and watched her. Even then he was beginning to suspect that there could be others.

As he climbed the stairs back to the deck, he lit the end of two sparklers: long, metallic cattails that buzzed and threw sparks every which way. He stuck one into the crack between the boat wall and door so the boy would see tiny stars shooting into the men's room.

"This man brought you something," the father said, his eyes still closed.

The door opened slowly. John Berry watched the kid, shirtless in cutoffs and tennis shoes, walk over and take the wire handle from him.

He wrote out words in orange cursive: *Bird, Sand,* a swirling *Water.* He announced each one.

Both flames went out then with a tired crackle and whiff. The boy eyed the box of sparklers in John Berry's pocket.

John Berry took three more out, lit them with his lighter, and passed one to the boy and another to his father, who put the handle into his mouth and shut his eyes. It made his face reddish and sparks tattered over the edge of his brow onto his bald head.

The boy wrote out his name, Billy, then his father's, Paul, then girls: Ann, Sue, Cathy . . .

John Berry tipped his and wrote *Emily* in the dark, etched it slowly, and saw it float there.

"Turn that shit off," Birdflower said, his hands moving over the grill like a magician.

Lila walked over to the cassette player which was balanced above the microwave and ejected a tape. "You wouldn't think you'd be so grumpy, now that you got yourself a girl."

Birdflower turned toward her and she thought she saw a smile edging up around his mouth.

The owner yelled out: "Three Fourth of July fish fries." She hustled to the grease bin, dropped the frozen fish patties into the metal basket, plopped them down with a sputter. Birdflower was wiping his face with a bandanna and sticking little toothpick American flags in a line of burgers.

"I don't know what your problem is lately," he said, shaking his head.

"I did it," she said casually. She waited for him to move. His wet T-shirt clung to his back. After a moment he turned his head and looked at her over his shoulder. "Did what?"

Lila walked over to him, leaned her stomach on the black knobs, and bent around, over the grill, so she could see his face. "You know," she said.

Birdflower flipped a hamburger, rolled the hot dogs, and pressed the cooked onions into a tighter pile.

Lila got closer to his face. "I said—"

"I get it," Birdflower said. "What do you want me to say?"

A kid screamed out on the porch and Lila moved away from him. "I don't know," she said, reaching for the prongs to get the fish. "I just thought you should know."

Emily wet a dish towel and put it on her neck and wrists. "There are millions out there. The seating list is two pages long. I never should have agreed to wait tables."

"You'll make good money for just wiggling your tail," Neal said.

She threw the towel across the counter at him.

"Very funny," he said, rocketing it back. "Your platters will be up in a minute."

Neal turned to check the scallops whitening in a skillet on the stove. The kitchen was damp with steam, and other waitresses hurried in and out without speaking to anyone.

She watched Eddie separating silverware into plastic canisters; knives, forks, soup spoons, the occasional long iced tea spoons all lay scattered under his hands. He'd worn jeans to work, and Emily knew that meant he was meeting Lila later.

The bell dinged and she walked over, set the broiled platters on the tray, twisted a lemon slice on each fish fillet, and grabbed a cocktail sauce cup for the shrimp. Over her shoulders she watched Eddie lobbing rinse tablets into the huge sinks. The water turned Caribbean blue in seconds.

Emily delivered the seafood and refilled water glasses. She saw about twenty old women in bright-colored pantsuits file into the dining room.

Some sat right down at the tables the busboy was pushing together for them. A few clustered around the entrance, rubbing their loose upper arms and pulling their jackets around them. Most of the women had gray hair tinted blue or purple and the styles were similar: short, with a loose curl on each side, and one lying like a little mouse on top.

She walked over and introduced herself to a few of the women at one end of the table and told them she'd be their waitress.

"We're the Georgia Songbirds," a big-breasted woman said. "We gave a concert down in Morehead." She was tanned on her forearms, as if from going onto the beach fully clothed.

Emily went around the table.

"My stomach," the last lady said, fingers clenching the menu, "is thinking of jumping clear out of my mouth and searching down food on its own." Emily wrote the order onto her pad. "Your tan is lovely," the woman said, and laid a pale hand on Emily's arm.

The big woman motioned to the others. All stood in a slow way, as for the Gospel in church, and began singing. Emily looked around at the other customers, and most smiled and nodded toward the women. "God bless America," they sang out. "Land that I love. Stand beside her, and guide her . . ."

The other waitresses paused around the coffee maker. They put their hands on their hips and shook their heads. For the first time that night, a few of them smiled. Eddie came out and stood beside the waitresses. Neal leaned in the doorway and placed a hand over his heart. The hungry woman at the end of the table began the next song with a voice like a young child's: "Yankee Doodle went to London riding on a pony . . ." The rest lifted their arms together and, with gusto, came in on the chorus, "I am that Yankee Doodle boy!"

"Usually I go down with my father in his truck," Lila said. "He always tells stories of other Fourths." They walked across a weedy lot toward the seawall. "How many pieces you got?" She pointed to the brown bag Eddie carried.

"Six," he said. Above them, the first white lights of fireworks.

Lila seemed a little nervous; her hands flittered while she talked on the walk over, and she wouldn't look at him, as she always did, directly in the eye. "Do they always start at midnight?" he said.

"Ever since I can remember." She held on to his arm and shook a pebble loose from her sandal, then she moved her hand. "Look," Lila said evenly. She stared at a point just past his face. "Did you get some things yet?"

Eddie nodded, his cheeks flushed.

"Not that I'm worried or anything," she said and kicked at the sandy dirt with the toes of her sandals. "I just wondered."

Eddie smiled. "Yeah, I got them at the gas station, in the men's room. They're called french tickle—"

"I don't want to hear about it," she said, and walked on.

A creeping greenish firework zipped up and burst.

They settled on the concrete sandbags—water nipped at their heels as they leaned their heads back so they could see the fireworks shooting up over the island. Eddie handed her a slice of watermelon. She took it in one hand and nibbled at the corner; a seed slipped off into the water. "Will we get drunk?"

"Maybe," Eddie said, mushing a bite in his mouth. "We put a

whole bottle in." He watched the horseshoe crabs wading in the shallow water, some joined together, others resting, sand edged up on their shells. They reminded Eddie of space bugs because of the way they moved in that small horrible way, rattails rotating behind.

Three red spinners went crazy, self-destructing in the sky.

Lila ate down to the rind. She flung the green smile out into the sound; it plopped and was gone. "I'm kinda worried," she said.

Eddie watched her eyes watch a few traveling sparks dissipate into the water. She had on a sleeveless white blouse, one Eddie knew had been her mother's. It had a stain up on one shoulder. She hugged her knees and rocked slightly. "Lila," Eddie said. She didn't answer, so he handed her another half-moon of pink melon.

She took it, laid it wetly on her shorts, and pressed a hand to her hair. "You know?" she said, and looked at him. "You know what I mean?"

Birdflower sat up on his elbow and filled Emily's cup with champagne. Both lay long-ways on a quilt spread out on the van floor.

Emily paused to watch the dark sky bloom with three yellow wheels of hissing light. "We eloped on a Friday night. He came and got me like a regular date. We crossed over the line and headed into Tennessee. I imagined the baby already kicking. We found this justice that ran a gas station—what I remember was the back room, yellow pine and girlie calendars all over."

Birdflower shook his head.

"Signed the divorce papers five years to the day," Emily said.

Birdflower drank from the big green bottle and put his palm on her stomach. "Plan it that way?" he asked.

"No. Things turn out," she said. "You know how it is."

Fireworks whizzed up. Emily put an arm around his hips and

pulled him forward. "Let's close the doors," she said. "Let's do it here."

John Berry swung himself around the dock post and splashed into the water. He moved his legs like riding a bicycle, treading water, watching the sky crackle and flare—the Fourth of July midnight finale was beginning.

From here he saw no one: no tourists cheering like morons, no locals or summer help who'd recognize him. He pulled his shoes off and threw them up onto the private dock, gulped air, and pushed his face under. He watched the last red, white, and blue gunpowder bursts from below the surface. Globes of light widening and shrinking, blurred and broken, like the image he'd seen when he jumped a minute earlier: his own face shifting in water.

NINE

THIS PLACE WAS REAL NICE

The bartender, playing his fingers across the glass bottles like piano keys, said, "We have Ancient Age, Beam's Blacklabel, Century Brooks, Fighting Cock, Jim Beam, Old Crow, Old Fitzgerald, Old Forrester, Rebel Yell, Sam Sykes, and Jack Daniel's Number 7."

John Berry's drink showed brown melting to clear, swirling like maple syrup. "Aw . . . just give me a beer," he said. The bartender sulked over to the tap and tilted a glass. He set it down in front of John Berry, the glass curved in the middle like a girl's waist.

"How was your Fourth?" the bartender asked.

"Okay," John Berry said.

"You back or just visiting?"

"Testing the waters."

The bartender wrapped plastic silverware in napkins and stood the white cocoons up in containers marked TAKE-OUT. John Berry thought he was intentionally trying to act busy. He didn't want to hear it, especially now in mid-afternoon when he wasn't making any money. John Berry knew that hundreds of men had sat on these bar stools and talked about women. He saw their female faces on the mirrored beer signs, smiling, pouting their bee-stung bottom lips. It didn't matter that much because he wouldn't say out loud what he'd decided anyway—that Emily was the love of his life. And that to ruin things, as he had, without trying to set them straight again would make him mean, crazy, and drunken forever. John Berry knew the bartender didn't trust him. He called him Blackbeard, and once last year he'd shown a painting of a pirate and pointed out to everybody who came into the bar for days how much it looked like John Berry. And it was true he had Edward Teach's blue-black hair and rubied cheekbones. He had the body type too, a mass of solid squares and rectangles placed against one another.

"You know, you look like shit," the bartender said.

"Why, thanks," John Berry said, and laughed awkwardly. He watched the beer sign left of the ice machine and slowly rubbed his palms against his knees. "There was this beauty queen in Norfolk," he started.

The bartender tucked a pencil behind his ear. "Is this some sleazy joke?"

"Nope," John Berry said. "I saw her in the mall. Standing in front of some formal-wear store passing out coupons. She had on this sequined dress that kind of shook. I sat on the edge of the fountain to watch her. I half thought she'd rise up and the ceiling would split open or else she'd run over to the falling water, dive, and become some kind of a mermaid or something."

"We don't see 'em like that around here," the bartender said.

"No. It was like she walked off the TV." Smoke spiraled up from the glass ashtray and the TV was turned low to soaps. Light fell in squares on the wood bar, across John Berry's shoulders, one side of his face, and on his arm lifting the glass.

"You off today?" the bartender said.

John Berry watched the bubbles break loose and float fast to the top of his beer. "Yeah, well, half day today. We pulled in at twelve and I walked off. Hitched a ride with three kids in a rusty VW. I could see the road through little holes under my feet."

The bartender shook his head. "So they just let you—"

"Tell me something. Who's she taking up with?" John Berry said.

The bartender picked up his empty glass. "I don't tell men who look as wild as yourself anything about their former women," he said. "All I do is pour the beers." He put the warm beer glass in a sink of water and John Berry heard it gently hit bottom.

"You can tell me who she's screwing," John Berry said, lifting off the stool.

"I haven't seen her," the bartender said evenly, drawing him another beer. "But I hear she's with that short-order cook from the Trolley."

"That long-hair," John Berry said. "For God's sake." He sat back on his stool.

"If you're down to make trouble," the bartender said, setting down the beer, "I'd think twice." He held out an open palm. "Look," he said. "Just because your sand castle washes down is no reason—"

"My goddamn life is not sand." John Berry clenched his beer, foam slipping over his fingers, and took it to the back table. He shouted behind him, "Just bring 'em to me when you see I'm empty—because that's your job."

· · ·

As he lifted the delicate spines from the flounder fillets that would be tonight's special, Birdflower daydreamed about trout fishing and how the first time he went he had waded in hip-high rubber down Black River in Michigan. Like any other hunter, he had searched, concentrating on dark patches of water. He could see them waving their tails in slow motion, cool pebbles on their bellies, giving a wide fish yawn. It had been his first time fly-fishing. He'd flipped the rod above his head, made it dance, and then, as his father told him, let the line drop just so, barely stinging the surface. Ahead, in the stream, his father looked over his shoulder and, as if from another world, smiled. And that was when he realized how alone he was and would probably always be. How the whole point of fishing was solitude. How his father had waited until he was old enough, until he saw him lying alone in his bedroom, eyes to the plaster swirls of the ceiling. He was *himself*, not his grade in school, his family, or his father. It was then that he realized he stood, taking up only the space—in the stream, on the land, and in the air—that he did.

"Six orders of strawberry pie to go," the owner shouted, fishing hat held at his hip.

Birdflower opened the fridge door and took out a pie of whole berries floating in red gelatin, molded by graham cracker crust. He cut each slice, snuggled them on Styrofoam plates, and covered them with Saran Wrap. They looked like road kills, Birdflower thought, watching the owner bag them and call out the window.

All day today he'd been thinking about Emily. He remembered when he'd heard the rumor that she swam nude every morning out at the point. One day, just after sunrise, he hid himself in the dunes. Sea oats blew figure eights that rustled against him. He watched her hold her hands up to the sun and splash up walls of slap-dash water. Her face changed continuously, smiles into whispers widening to laughs. He watched as she somersaulted and twisted. It was then that he fell half in love with her, and decided he wanted her for himself.

The owner stepped around the corner.

"The rush is over; you can clear out of here," he said, pushing his hat back on his bald head. He looked at him hard a minute. "I just want to warn you. These island guys. They're different from you or me. When they were growing up, they never saw cities with one-way streets or highways where you had to stay in your lane. You know what I mean? They've never seen a parking cop, a paddy wagon, or a big state pen from a car window. You've heard them . . . they all think they're pirates."

"With no brains," Birdflower laughed. He took out his cigarettes from his shirt pocket and checked to see how many were left. "When's the last time you had a girl?"

The owner winked. "Besides my wife, you mean? Oh, one hundred, maybe two hundred years."

Birdflower smiled and opened the door into the dull sunlight. He walked out onto the back porch.

"Okay," the owner called after him. "All I'm saying is those fellows aren't for messing with."

"Uh-huh," Birdflower said. He unbuttoned his shirt and pulled one of the cigarettes out of the pack with his teeth. To him John Berry seemed almost comical, living on the ferry and existing on six-packs and vending machine candy. Birdflower shaded his eyes. He shouldn't have thrown the bottle, but God knows he had his reasons. Birdflower puffed his dangling cigarette and arched against the boards. He thought he understood. He knew Emily's body and how you wanted to climb into it. She had a lazy way that made everyday life fluid and easy. He pushed a cheek against the cooling weathered wood. Still, the bottom line was that only savages cut women. He flicked his cigarette to the sand and took the steps by twos, walking quickly towards Paolo's for a couple after-work beers.

・ ・ ・

The bar had filled—a guitar player sang Jackson Browne songs on the raised stage, and the waitress was lighting candles at each table. John Berry burped quietly. His empty basket, chips and pickle, rustled as he reached for crumbs. He was going through all the cottages on the island, remembering curtains, front yards, birdbaths or planters, trying to fade the nausea and loneliness of being back to a place you know completely but feel a stranger to. He was thinking of a time when he was a kid and he and his younger brother—who now lived off the island and was continually coming for vacations with some bookish woman who hated the sun but loved the people and wrote down everything obsessively in bound journals—had collected every can and bottle on the whole island. They nagged their father to drive to spots way up the beach road that they couldn't ride their bikes to. He remembered trading in these bottles and ordering from the back of *Life* magazine with the money. The ad showed a boy with a buzzcut and a happy face in an air-propelled minicar. When it came, they spent days assembling it, careful of every weight-conscious detail. The day finally came, and John Berry and his brother carried it out to the flat grass in the backyard all the time talking about the Wright brothers. They flipped a coin and it was his brother who solemnly stepped in and ignited the engine, and for one brief boyhood moment John Berry saw him, shoulders and head above the floating contraption and the slight lift and pause on that morning so many summers ago.

Over the bar the TV flashed a vampire movie. Dracula passed through a hanging fern. John Berry watched the count's cape flutter, blood dripped from his lips. He felt Emily's lips on his neck, then the tug and pull, till he was dizzy and his eyes would roll white. John Berry's head jerked to where Birdflower was ordering a beer with a nod at the bar. That long-hair was skinny; frying burgers didn't give you muscles. He could kill him if he wanted.

The bartender pointed back and Birdflower glanced over his shoulder as if alone at night and hearing footsteps.

People around him quieted, looked back, and shifted nervously in their seats. One woman took her baby from the high chair to her lap. The bartender walked over and said, "No bar fights. I swear I'll call the sheriff in a heartbeat."

John Berry stared dead-eyed at his beer. "Tell that hippie I won't touch him. I just want to know a few things."

"I'll pass the message on," the bartender said.

"Before you shits got here, either raising your motels or working in them, this place was real nice." John Berry sat across from Birdflower, who listened, his eyes tied to the tiny reflection of himself in his bottle. "I grew up in a house on Howard Street. You know what happened? Some idiot bought it from my mother. Painted it yellow. And is calling it the Canary Guest Cottage."

"Why'd you throw the bottle?" Birdflower said.

"There's not a person I see in the winter months crossing that I don't know," John Berry continued.

Through straggles of loose hair, Birdflower was looking him over.

"If you think this has nothing to do with you, asshole, you're wrong."

Birdflower stood up. "Man, you're nuts."

"Sit down," John Berry said, standing and pushing him back into his chair. The bartender made a warning sign. John Berry held up his hand. "Okay, okay," he said.

Birdflower stood. "Any other words of wisdom you'd like to lay on me before I go."

Creepy Dracula music played and John Berry threw back his head like a crazy person. "She'll leave you, too," he said. "You fucking guru."

· · ·

Alone on the road Birdflower counted his ribs carefully like a child doing scales. Headlights flashed in a parade of beach jeeps and trucks heading to the bar. He stuck his hands deep in his pockets and walked barefoot in the loose sand at the side of the road. He lost his balance and fell. Sharp gravel pushed into his palms and his knees grated against the asphalt. Standing, he brushed his hands and ran barefoot toward the restaurant.

Hidden by the low cedars near the storage shed, he watched her. The bright lights of the kitchen showed her arm ladling soup. He saw her face muted behind the screen's haze.

Nothing was wrong. Safe in the kitchen, she was working for Neal, who had an old boyfriend here for the weekend. She was even dressed in the cutoffs he had left wedged down in the covers of her bed. Birdflower lit a cigarette. They were going together to Norfolk in a few days. Things would settle. She was with *him*, not John Berry, who was just an ignorant old island boy way out of his league.

It was obvious to Birdflower that she didn't want John Berry, that her fascination with the backward lives of the islanders was over. Though he hadn't known her long, Birdflower convinced himself that they had similar desires, and that he was better suited for her because he understood free love.

Gnats circled his head: she would stay with him. Birdflower watched her put onions in an unseen frying pan—heard the snap and sizzle and imagined the blue gas flame. Moving back into the shadows, he watched her step out and head for the walk-in. Behind the veil of cold smoke she chose things. When she came out she gazed at the night sky. Birdflower looked up with her at a star showing through moving clouds.

"Just once," John Berry said, pressing a hand on the wheel.

"No way," Tom said.

"I won't get out of the car. I'll just see if any lights are on."
Tom looked at him.

"Come on," he said. "I'm begging you."

"You'll come to my house then? Susan will fix up the couch."

"Yep," John Berry said, sipping the beer he'd snuck out of Paolo's under his shirt.

Tom shifted down and rounded the corner, then down once more as the car pumped onto the sandy street. They passed the two-trunked maple tree and the dilapidated shack where John Berry knew the island kids smoked dope. The other houses leading to Emily's were dark.

"Turn off the lights," John Berry said as he hunkered down. His wobbly finger pointed through the glass. "Her cottage is there."

"Nobody's home," Tom said. "I didn't drive down here to chauffeur you around."

"Shut up," John Berry said, watching the sneakers, crab nets, and clam racks, sprawled all over her front porch. A sudden glow came on from inside the bedroom. "She's lit a candle," he whispered.

Tom moved the car forward, its tires muffled in the sand. Neither spoke till the car was speeding up the island highway, a splinter of moon above. "They're lemon-scented," John Berry said as he watched the waves beat against the sand.

TEN

NORFOLK

W e're outta here," Birdflower said, his hands on the wheel. "This island doesn't bother me in the winter, but when the tourists start coming out of the woodwork . . ." He shook his head and noticed the tall birds wading in Sugar Creek to their left. Wind sprayed from window to window. Emily watched the town end of the island fade till it was only a few slanted roofs and the top half of the lighthouse. Not since she borrowed John Berry's truck to pick up Eddie in Norfolk had she been off the island. She had been late and he was standing out-side, his duffel bag by his feet, leaning against a phone booth. His

voice high and breathless, "I thought you'd forgotten me," he
said.

Birdflower zoomed the tape deck fast forward to a whiny finish.
He lit a cigarette and plugged the lighter back in. "What if he's on
here?"

"He won't be," she said, her fingertips tracing a seagull-shaped
scar at her temple. "Nothing will happen." Her eyes were focused
on the back of the car in front of them, packed so tightly with
clothing that a few boxes of cereal and crackers seemed to float up
to the glass.

Emily sat in a back booth—a famous landmark map of North
Carolina above her head. Birdflower watched her from his spot in
line. Fluorescent lights made her skin look olive and patchy. She
didn't take the mainland well. Two bare-chested boys in shorts
danced near her with a helium balloon. They held it down, then
let it go, laughing each time it floated back up. At a table close by,
a surfer snuggled with his remarkably pale girlfriend.

Behind the counter a girl bagged burgers. In front of Birdflower
was a man and his little girl in a blue bathing suit with a flounced
skirt. The cashier pushed his tray forward and the child followed
like a duck.

Emily caught his eye, smiled, waved.

Birdflower smiled back, then turned to order. On the ferry trip
she'd kept her eyes on the empty cans and paper on the van's
floor. She'd shifted in her seat and pinched the skin on her thigh.
He'd tried to calm her, offered her weed, played the slow ballads
on all his tapes, and finally asked her about being pregnant. It was
then that she settled herself and talked quietly about sensations,
moods, and how her hair had changed from yellow-white to a tone
like goldenrod.

Birdflower listened, but he was preoccupied. He'd seen the fer-
rymen glare at the van and talk among themselves. He'd watched

her and thought how important it was she stay with him. He was worried because he knew styles of men changed with the times. For a while he had been in fashion, sensitive, intuitive; but now women wanted other qualities, discipline, sternness, and money. On the mainland, his situation had been dismal, and that was why Emily seemed so crucial—she didn't seem to care that he'd gone completely out of style.

"This is so weird," Emily said when he'd sat down. "All these people so close to you."

"Seems a little barbaric," Birdflower said. He unwrapped his burger.

"But you miss it," Emily said. "I mean, these skinny french fries, and who could make a burger like this?" She held up her bun—mustard and ketchup mixed like an ink blot. "Like you could eat one of these anywhere."

"Comfort in that?" Birdflower asked.

"Kind of," Emily said, squirting a ketchup pack all over her fries.

The clerk handed him the aqua key ring. "We've tracked people down as far as Texas for stealing stuff. You can have the Bible. But the rest is ours."

Emily walked out of the motel's office and up the curling cement stairs. On the second floor, Birdflower slipped an arm around her waist. His eyelids looked heavy.

At the first convenience store after the McDonald's—which they had not stopped at but still somehow seemed a marker for him—Birdflower had pulled a rolled plastic bag from under the seat. He puffed, spoke in a held-breath voice, and let the smoke blow against the glass. He turned up his tapes, and again and again raced the reverse to familiar guitar riffs. It wasn't that she didn't like getting high, she appreciated the easing, the slight numbing sensation, the way time lost parameters, and how touch-

ing became central and diaphanous as air. But she didn't think
Birdflower should smoke so much and he'd gotten so stoned on
the trip she'd felt like the only sober one at a drunken high school
party.

Her thonged sandal sucked cement. "Why so fast, baby?" Birdflower said, grabbing her arm. He looked like a retarded man:
same slow eyes she'd seen once on a man watching girls pass on
the beach.

Outside their door, the pink motel sign came on with a neon
click and buzz. "I'm sorry," Birdflower said. "I'll flush it all if you
want." He put the key in Emily's palm.

She thought of the dusty ride and the ache in the back of her
thighs. "I'm taking a bath. Why don't you go get some beer?"

She left Birdflower sitting on the orange-flowered bedspread
drawing lines around a blossom. "No more," she heard him say as
the water beat into the motel tub.

"I like bottles," she yelled, unzipping her jeans, yanking them
off by the bottom and testing the water with a long first toe. She
pulled her T-shirt off.

Emily settled into the bath, her nipples, belly, and knees floating above water like islands. The island's own well water was too
rich in iron for soaking. It stained her skin and left her hair tinted
red. Steam rose and water rocked against her hips. She remembered failed vacations from her marriage. The trip would turn as
reasonlessly as wind drifts over water: a bad dinner, a flat tire, or a
forgotten hairbrush and the whole thing would be ruined. It was
harder for them because they lived a vacation.

She turned over on her stomach and thought of the first trip
she'd ever taken with Daniel, how she'd wanted it to go well. It
was just over the border that she'd mentioned flowers and he'd
looked oddly at her, and asked where he was supposed to get
them. She'd smudged daisies with her pinky over the window. He
pulled over and they looked in the brush on the side of the road.
She found two tattered daisies. He found a few fisted morning

glories that looked like tissue paper when he held out his hand. Soon after, he had taken a flashlight and gone into the woods. She waited in the car thinking of the irises on the dark side of her parents' house and the big silky petaled magnolia in the backyard. He returned with nothing and they drove on toward the town they had heard of with the judge who would marry you for five dollars.

The door clicked. "Me," Birdflower said. A bag rustled and then there was a little gasp from a twist-off beer. Birdflower walked into the bathroom and put a green bottle near her on the tub's edge. He sat across the paper banner of the closed toilet seat. Emily tipped her beer up.

Birdflower looked at his beer, then let his eyes slowly peruse her body. "I want this to be good," he said. "I've been thinking about it every other minute for days."

"Have you ever noticed when you're off, it's always like you're a silver minnow in a plastic cup or something?" she said, water lapping back and forth from her toes to her neck.

"We're in the same cup," he said as he moved to sit on the ledge. He kissed her and with a finger drew a line on her neck up to her ear. His hand moved over her wet hair, which separated and dripped at the shoulders.

Emily thought, *I'll stay with you as long as I can.*

He sat on the bed watching Emily put lotion on her newly shaven legs. She had on a calico sundress and different leather sandals than usual. He was dressed up too, white shirt, open paisley vest, and his jeans were the newer of the two pair he owned. He drank the last beer. It was weird that just two months ago on his birthday in May he had been so alone. He'd woken early and smoked a joint in bed, watching the tip blend with the rising sun out his window. He made a cake, this year devil's food, sometimes angel: a tradition his mother had started, depending on the behavior of the year. Later, after a quiet day of meditation on his life's odometer turning over, he had dinner and a slice of his cake. When he had finished, pushed his plate forward, and sat back to light a cigarette, he felt that something would have to happen very soon.

"Ready?" she said.

"To hit the town with you," Birdflower said.

When they got in the van, Emily brushed sand off the seat as though she'd never seen the stuff. He saw them at some low-ceilinged, red-lighted club, fishbowl drinks in front of them with mermaid swizzle sticks. They were quiet and he started thinking about the little house on Lake Michigan his father had left him. A friend had told him a small village had grown up at water's edge. Lately he envisioned them in the back of some bakery there. Her chopping nuts for bread, him pouring batter into muffin tins. He'd told her this a few days ago. She was not as enthusiastic as he had hoped. That scared him. He knew she was like a plant and he worried that if he brought her up there, to the frozen ground, it'd be all over. She might get limp and start asking for water and before you knew it, one morning he would wake up to find a pile of dry leaves next to him in bed. On Ocracoke the cold was different. It blew off the sea instead of moving up from the earth the way it did in the upper peninsula. Last year he'd seen the winter ocean. He'd been stoned and drunk and decided around four in the afternoon to borrow a speedboat and take a look. The water was navy-black and the moving whitecaps reminded him of an old guy's fingertips coming together and then apart, as though the ocean was wringing its hands. Even the few coal-black fish that jumped were shivering: their breath making tiny puffs over the water.

They chose the place because it was red-barn color and had a chain of pink elephants across one side. The bouncer took their money. "Have you seen stuff like this before?" He turned the bill up so that Lincoln eyeballed Emily's breasts.

"Yeah, man. She's seen it all," Birdflower said.

The air conditioner hummed and bubbled, filtered and cooled the place as though it was underwater. They let their eyes focus on the wood tables. Birdflower watched the light and movement of the blinking Busch river, the neon Budweiser clocks, and the giant can of Michelob lit on the far wall. As if each had accidentally floated there, lone men scattered the bar. They chose a table and Birdflower left Emily fingering candle wax at the back.

"Piña Coladas are the only faggy drinks we serve," the bartender said. With his thick fingers he poured powder into a silver shaker. Birdflower looked to a shallow pool in front of the bar. He threw down ten bucks. "You keep fish in that center thing?"

"That there," the bartender said, "is for mud wrestling."

Birdflower saw the sheen off the smooth mud. "Big guys?"

The bartender set the drinks down, each with a half-opened paper umbrella. "No," he said. "Girls. Real live girls."

On their way to this place, the full moon had sometimes seemed to race the car, other times falling back beyond the trees. It reminded her of the things she'd said, in June, she'd try to figure out. During the varied phases she *had* thought some. But it was hard for Emily to yank herself into thinking like that. Her life worked by brief exchanges. It was a twisting, swerving thing that formed in a familiar but always somewhat remarkable way. The moon had appeared then, and she realized this: No man could save you from any other man. Birdflower was no solution, as she'd been trying to convince herself, for her fear of John Berry.

Birdflower came back with the drinks and sat down. A couple squeezed into the table near them. Emily sucked her straw. The woman was fat, had on blue bell-bottoms and a shirt tied at the midriff with a white tube top underneath. When she saw women like this, so obviously confident with themselves but so different from herself, Emily tried to figure out where she fit in the long arch of females. She saw it like some kind of rainbow, spread not with thin color but with millions of different women. She looked down at her knees, the rough scar like a wild berry on her right and the burn from the lowest rack of the restaurant stove on the left.

Her eyes caught two women in small red bikinis coming out a door near the bar along with a big striped referee penguin walking behind.

"They're going to wrestle," Birdflower said. He pointed to the threesome lining up by the pit. She watched the women do muscle poses. The referee touched the mud and winked at the men in the front. Emily stared at the small sequined suits. "They look my age," she said. "You can tell by that crepe paper skin on their upper arms."

A whistle blew and the jukebox slackened mid-song. Birdflower looked embarrassed. He was opening and closing his own little umbrella. The two women stepped into the mud, arms out like sumo wrestlers. There were tentative ringside shouts of encouragement.

Birdflower pulled her wrist forward so their heads met in the middle of the table. "We can leave." Emily shook her head. Men around her were lifting off their chairs. Smoke from their cigarettes was backlit by the red net candles on every table. More men lined up against the walls, long-neck beers held with a finger in their belt loop.

"I want to see this," Emily said. She had said that same thing years ago about a porno flick her husband had rented for a bachelor party. He had reluctantly set the projector on a chest of drawers in their bedroom. Lights off. A little square over the bed no bigger than a TV screen. And many men around one woman, at all angles, moving in a variety of directions like some out-of-whack machine. At the end Emily left the room. She made no comment, but it stayed with her. Later that night as she moved her husband onto her, she closed her eyes and somehow felt what she'd seen all over her body and then imagined more than one man with her and for an instant it was simple; she was a functional organ. Like a heart pumping.

Emily sunk lower. She watched the women down in the mud roll onto each other. The mud oozed through their toes, under their arms, and gathered in their hair. One was down and there was a two-beat chant from the back tables and then a roar as both women twisted like water moccasins. Emily braced her hands on the table; she felt as if she were being sucked into the mud. She saw herself in the pit: brown mud hiding the everyday her, letting her become someone only her body knew. With their strong arms the women pulled at her waist, kneeled over her, and pinned her arms. When she tired and looked into the face above, she found that it was her own muddied features. She jerked. The woman pressed up to her lips and kissed her. The room was only dim red light as her other self disappeared into the mud.

The crowd cheered. Emily watched the girls in the ring claw and kick. The dark-haired one straddled the other. Emily felt the mud squish between her stomach and another's. Both arched up into familiar pinup poses. The referee circled like a dazed bear.

Birdflower grabbed her hand as people all around started to stand. He shouted, "Baby, let's go somewhere civilized." Emily heard this, but just smiled and ran a finger down the curve of her cleavage. She was already wriggling in the mud. There were other shapes approaching her, moving on her. Emily watched the women push each other's face into the mud. One wrestled the other's top off. Emily fingered the nipple of her breast. The muddy top was held up like a caught fish. The chanting was louder and Birdflower's hand tightened on hers. He used his head to signal toward the door. The cheering voices were like an ocean. *You can't tell them apart,* she was thinking. *They could be anyone.* She could see only through a mass of men's legs and around their hips, a jungle of body parts. Slithering like some new animal, she found her way, feeling the mud on her neck and between her legs. She'd slip off her dress and roll till, if she lay still, no one could find her. Only her light eyelashes would rise out of the mud like seedlings. She was very close. Only a few men to pass. She went slowly, squirming all her parts forward.

A hand tightened on her arm. "Where the hell do you think you're going?"

She knew him and watched him carefully through slit eyes as he pulled her through the crowd toward the exit sign.

Emily did a dead man's float in the motel pool. The moon was like an earring she once lost. Inside, Birdflower was lulled in sleep by the air conditioner's steady breath. She'd come out to stand on the diving board and do an easy striptease, T-shirt then panties floating near her like huge petals. Lazily she lifted her head for air and saw herself in an aquarium, a fish floating sideways, cloudy-eyed on top.

There were plate-sized lights underwater. A NO DIVING AFTER MIDNIGHT sign, scattered lawn chairs, and a vista of two long double-decker rows of motel rooms, clipped shrubs, and the late night stars above. Emily preferred the ocean—she backstroked from blue ceramic side to side—but this was nice, clean water on her skin; her body a showpiece, a trained porpoise doing laps. She floated, toes arched skyward, and sank into an underwater somersault. Because her mouth was dry, she sidestroked to the spigot under the diving board. There was one childhood moment she always remembered. She'd walked to the rabbit cage the neighbors had in their backyard. Inside the mother rabbit had been slouched over, showing her nipples, a baby rabbit attached to each one. Off to the side, there had been a dead one covered with a dozen flies. One of that rabbit's eyes gazed loosely into the straw. And she'd stood there at six or seven, her hands climbing into her shirt for her own nipples. *This is me,* she thought and turned her head up to the sky.

Emily left the spigot and dived underwater. Swimming along the bottom, her belly grazed the pool floor like a blue-gray shark.

She floated on her back: body down five inches, head a mask above water. She had seen Eddie walking barefoot along the main road with Lila. He'd dropped her hand when he saw Emily's car. She spread her arms and legs out wide like angels in snow. Maybe now he was on the beach with her, their hair blown back from their faces, Eddie's head flipping from the moon to the girl's blouse whipped tight around her. She had to be careful what she said to Eddie about girls, because her feelings were irrational; she felt jealous and oddly suspicious of the intentions of a local girl like Lila.

Emily rolled over and over like a kid circling down a hill. John Berry might be on the ferry tomorrow. His face was unclear. She remembered now just a vague beefiness around his upper thighs and the coarse quality of his hair.

Emily held to the side and kicked small tight scissor cuts. As though it was boiling, the water bubbled around her. Birdflower opened the door of the room and stood by the small outside light in his underwear, his long braid over one shoulder like a girl's. He climbed down the stairs, cleared the metal fence, and squatted by the pool's edge. She saw his body pinprickle as he lowered himself in and with one hand loosened the band of his braid.

"Let's not go back," he said.

Emily laughed and splashed water at him. She swam to the darkest edge of the pool.

In a quick head-thrown-freestyle he trailed her, cornering her, and pressed his body against hers. Emily's back rubbed tiles.

"No way," she said.

"Come on," he said.

"Everybody lives on an island." Their wet heads bobbed above water. Emily said, "Some just aren't out in the ocean."

"You're so profound," Birdflower said, his hands resting on each side of her rear.

Open-mouthed and falling, Emily kissed him. She saw at eye's edge a light flicker on in the first-floor row of rooms and a man at the window, looking up to the unanimous night sky and then holding a drink high as if in a toast to her.

ELEVEN

MERIDIAN

Wind moved the small Cape Hatteras office. John Berry flipped photos like cards into the circle of light in the middle of the room. He shuffled to one of himself and Emily on the beach, beers in hand and a bonfire in the background. Her face was flushed and her hair fell into a center part and blew slightly forward. That night, everyone had been so drunk around the fire, singing songs and one guy telling about times he went out on a late-night shrimper with his father, and how the trollers would gather around the boat with the best storyteller, and how that man's voice would whisper into the scene of lantern lights nodding from boat to boat. Near sunrise, John Berry had awoken with Emily's full weight on top of him and he'd carried her to the truck as the sun inched up. He folded the photograph. The next was of him and his father, both in Bermuda shorts, standing in Wanchese Harbor. That was the last time his father had been off the island before he died. For a minute John Berry looked into the tiny eyes of his dad and was oddly lonely for him. But his father had not minded dying. Earlier in his life he'd said right out that he'd seen more change on the island, and in the world, than his father had and probably more than John Berry ever would. At the graveyard, on a bright June morning, one which seemed to take away all the gloomy corners and uncertainties of death, John Berry had stood near his father's grave, and as the first shovel of dirt was pitched down, he threw in a handful of white sand. It sprayed up like the points of a wave, dazzled, then landed—pelting the coffin hundreds of times.

His thumb pressed on the gloss of a large one—Emily red-eyed from the flash, in a green halter dress, her glass held up for New Year's Eve. Around her waist were four creeping fingers. He held the photo near his hand to see if they matched. There was a hint of stray knuckle hairs—but how could he really tell? He threw the photo. It flipped backwards and flapped down. Pulleys rang against the flagpole and the aluminum office hissed.

John Berry checked the windows, no cars yet on his side. The green and red channel markers blinked out in the water and beyond he saw the dim winking lights of the island. A van's high beams threw light on John Berry's face and showed his finger pulling down a venetian blind. The lights flipped off and the van's engine rattled.

He looked into the shoe box; shiny bits of color were mixed and jumbled in the rectangle as if his whole life was the turning end of a kaleidoscope. Looking out at the two people in the van, he saw that they were kissing, and before long, he realized it was them.

The tick of the clock beat out pairs of seconds as Emily snuggled her head onto Birdflower's shoulder. A camper pulled in behind the van and a sleepy-looking woman tipped ashes from her cigarette out the window.

He'd get the pellet gun from the truck, shove it into his pocket, and force Birdflower to swim out and grab the last dock pole. Then he'd get into the van and drive Emily over the water to the white house, to their life as it had been.

He gathered the pictures off the carpet. The ferry was maneuvering its mass into the dock. John Berry slipped out of the back, gently resting the door behind him. The deep ferry whistle sounded. He got in his truck and inched the door closed, ignited the engine, and flipped the gear shift into reverse. In snapshots, John Berry envisioned the next scenes, one after another, blurred and hectic. The wheels of the truck straightened and he headed for the curving line of cars.

John Berry stood above the deck, his beige windbreaker making an empty rustle. He watched them talk. In the solitude of swishing wind and water he rehearsed his speech to her. Lines he'd written on scraps of paper for a month formed themselves on his lips.

A light in the van went on and the hippie got out and walked starboard like a drunken Indian against the wind. John Berry bolted to the deck, passed a line of orange preservers on the white wall, and paused at the van's door.

She saw not what she expected—Birdflower back to draw her into the big pink sky—but John Berry, and her hands went up to cover her face from the memory of the bottle and the glass spindrift. He got in and she pressed her body against the door. Through her fingers she saw him in long fractures.

"I'm sorry," he said.

She lowered her hand. Seeing the cuts, he reached to her temple and brushed the tiny speckled ones shaped like seeds. She flinched, and he took his hands back and rested his forehead— rough hair everywhere—on the wheel. "I want to come home," he whispered. Wind sputtered through the windows.

"Well, you can't." She heard her voice reverberate off the front window, the floor, and the bucket seats.

"Please," he said.

She shook her head. "Too much has happened."

"Bullshit," he said.

"Get out," she said in a tired voice.

He placed a hand on her face. With his fingertips he stroked the curve of her neck, and made her ease and press against his hand. "Let me come back," John Berry said.

Emily didn't answer. His hand firmed around her neck, and he said it again slowly. She rolled her head.

"I might kill you," he said and opened the door, all the time thinking, *What is this? what now?* "Those scars," he said. "One for every man."

Birdflower watched John Berry run from the van into the metal archway and down into the bowels of the boat. He saw Emily's startled face through the glass and knew he should give her a moment. John Berry's rounded shoulders had looked like his own. It was as though he had watched himself scurry away. Her past lives moved and changed, spit out stories, made her wild some days and quiet some nights. The curtains which somehow delineated past and present would part and from the backstage of her life a player would come to add some scattered scene.

Birdflower opened the van door. His hands moved across the eternity of the front seat. Their fingers meshed and she pulled him back in.

· · ·

John Berry's ears rang. It was the way he thought atom bombs would sound: a falling hiss then a long tone signaling the end. Behind his temples he felt a red ache which sent thin spears of color to his eyelids. He kept forgetting if he loved her or hated her. Ahead, the van circled Silver Lake inlet and rattled out of sight. They're going to the long-hair's house. John Berry slowed. "Let 'em," he said. "Let 'em get stoned and eat wheat crackers."

He flipped the wheel and headed down the sand road, thinking up confrontations. She never spoke, just came in and stood there with the corners of her mouth set and her hands dangling as if weightless and blown against her thighs.

In her driveway he turned off the engine and left the truck. The air smelled early. The screen door banged behind him. Everything was as it had been. He moved through the house, stopping at each doorway. He paused at her bedroom. Through the branches of a hunchback cedar, leaf-light moved on the pillow and the bed made with a crazy quilt: thunder-shaped patches of red flannel and heart-like pieces of men's dress pants. The same posters of black girls with flowers in their hair and palm trees and huts behind them. He rested on the bed. Collected in a box near the door were his razor, belt buckle, and flashlight. He thought of her quite casually picking up something of his—maybe the ivory-handled brush—and begin to move the bristles through her hair, but the handle would heat up as she realized it was his, and she'd drop it and kick it over to the box, get a rag, and carefully, holding it away from her body, put it in.

On the bed he found the way he liked to sleep best, one arm behind her head and the other snuggled under her waist. He scanned the room from his cheek-flat position. His blue pants, a pair he had trouble getting into, were slung over the chair. The hippie wears them, he thought. He sat up, went to the dresser, and began dumping drawers. He saw her, in the doorway, then on the bed. With one hand he whipped across the dresser, spraying her perfume, hair combs, and creams against the wall. He thought he saw her face in the mirror and her image moving in photos stuck along the edge. Her lips were telling him things she didn't know, listing his secrets, his crazy thoughts. Faster, her voice high now, hissing into a sound like rushing water. With his teeth he tore a hole the size of his fist between the legs of her pants.

"Hey," Eddie said from the doorway. "What are you doing?"

"I came to get my stuff," John Berry said.

"You gave my mother scars."

"And you better believe she gave some to me."

"You could have killed her," Eddie said.

John Berry pulled the quilt off the bed and stuffed it into the pillowcase. "Get out of my way," he said as he threw the bag over his shoulder.

"You're a prick," Eddie said.

At first impulse John Berry held a hand up to slap him, but he saw Eddie was shaking and he moved around the boy. The bright light from the door gave them both grainy auras, made their movements seem blurry and slow. He walked out of the house, one foot on the shaded cement steps, then the other on the next, and out across the yard. He climbed inside his truck and started the engine.

"She's better than all of you," Eddie screamed from the porch.

As John Berry turned from the loose sand driveway onto the gravel road, he watched the boy in the rearview mirror. Eddie was leaning against the cottage, sliding down like a water drop on glass, his arms wrapped around himself.

Feeling sorry now, John Berry pushed the horn and raised his hand. He waved, waited, but Eddie would not look up. He felt angry at Eddie. His face reddened, he pressed the gas pedal and spun out, throwing up pebbles into the morning sky.

TWELVE

THE VEGETABLE TRUCK

I t *was* too early in the day for mosquitoes, but Emily could see the rain puddles quivering irregularly with the laying and hatching and hovering of them. All night it had rained, at one point so hard she'd been sure water would puddle around Bird-flower's door, and she'd gotten up heavily, still tired from the drive back from Norfolk, and stuffed rags underneath the edges. The mosquitoes sometimes got so bad after a storm that the park service sprayed. A ranger drove around a truck that shot out intermittent streams of pink smoke that settled on everything and smelled like a mix of perfume and ash.

She walked up the beach road, toward the spot where the vegetable truck parked. She wanted strawberries, had wanted them for months. Each week the man promised he'd have some next time, and would try selling her blueberries or bruised raspberries. Once even a stray bag of cranberries. Emily leaned up against the farthest end of the pony pen, near the road. She put a leg behind her on a rung. Haze was burning off the highway and she could see triangles of sun on the water at the horizon.

The vegetable man always reminded her of Daniel. To her he looked like the actor in the movies who was always the leading man's best friend, the one with more integrity and sensitivity than the lead, just a bit sloppier and more vulnerable.

Daniel had stayed in bed late on the weekends and drank wine with her. Once he made her a necklace out of tobacco seeds and he always dried some rose petals from the front bushes for her bath. He said that it was only because of her that he could farm, that otherwise he would have been a teacher or a minister.

She half believed someday it would be Daniel asking her if she wanted green grapes or red ones. Maybe that was why she was always the first, able to choose the loveliest of everything. Though sometimes, self-conscious of the island women whispering around her, she'd intentionally buy bruised peaches, browned bananas, lettuce that would soon be worthless. She knew what they were saying, in their patterned housedresses and awkward hairdos. That she was a poor mother and untrue to the people who were stupid enough to love her. The kinder ones might say she was confused, scattered, that she had been disillusioned early, and that this life was the best she could manage.

Every few years there'd be a guy who thought he could really figure her out. "You seem like a person who's been hurt badly," he'd say. And she told him, no, she'd just come to the conclusion sooner than most, that absolute happiness wasn't possible. The husband, baby, house formula didn't figure and she'd decided that if she couldn't be happy she'd at least do what she wanted. Emily would further explain that absolute despair wasn't possible. They'd always relent for a while before telling her she seemed distant. Not distant physically, they never meant that. They just couldn't understand her lack of interest in their educated intellects, in their world travels. She could count the Indo-China stories she'd heard, Malaysia with a French girl who wore her hair short and had a pair of little round John Lennon glasses. The tattered children in Costa Rica, the way when you were robbed in Latin America they even took your half bar of soap, and how in Berlin the Germans yelled at you to get back if you attempted to cross before the red walking man changed to green. She remembered how she would block them out by listening to her irises knock thickly against the house.

The ferry horn sounded, and minutes later, the vegetable truck appeared, small and blurry up the highway. It looked good beating back the telephone poles. Today there would be strawberries and she would walk back with them along the beach, stopping at a stretch across from Sugar Creek. There the water swung up in a half ellipse and smoothed the sand to a curve as fine as skin. These highs and lows reminded her of the hip, thigh, and stomach of some contorted giant. And she would sit there, snuggled into that lovely passage between groin and upper thigh, and eat her strawberries, cut them thin as petals with the pocket knife she carried and lay each slowly on her tongue.

THIRTEEN

NUDE MOON

ouring rain. Emily held a newspaper over her head. It sagged at the edges like a nun's habit and gray ran off in lines down her fingers. As she walked barefoot back from the beach through deep puddles, sand stuck to her ankles in delicate, lace-like patterns. In the drier inner landscape of her mind, Emily thought about lies. Rain shook the leaves. She had always lied easily, switched fact for fiction, embroidered stories with her own thread. It wasn't really lying though, just her physical knowledge of cycles; a vague familiarity with events that had yet to happen. She believed in omens and often waited before doing things for signs of weather. It was important to recognize an indigo sky, the few clouds at noon collecting into definable shapes, or the late afternoon mist, which reminded her of time-lapse film of seeds sprouting and most specifically that moment when seedlings threw off the dust on their new leaves and grew toward the sky.

Emily let the paper fall to the porch. Through the rain she saw the beach towels and bathing suits soaked on the line outside and water pounding down from the gutters. In the kitchen she turned the spigot on, bent down, and drank. Water blown through the screen door had gathered in puddles around the floor.

He had been here. She looked into the bedroom. Below the windows, rain dripped into drawers dumped out and scattered.

"Eddie," she called, then ran to his empty room. She walked quickly back to her bed. A car lumbered past. She pressed her spine against the wooden headboard, drew her knees to her chest.

Evening was coming on fast. The rain beat a hectic rhythm on the roof. Shadows of water melted and moved like a lava lamp over the walls. She ran her tongue over a childhood scar on her knee. It tasted oddly tinny and the tissue was pinker, the color of cooked salmon and slightly raised like braille.

She lifted her head and looked around the room. In her closet, a triangle was torn from the crotch of a pair of pants. Emily carefully walked over and turned on the overhead light. It made each scattered object impossibly real. Flipping the light off, she stood in the doorway and watched the shifting shadows.

"Mom," Eddie yelled from the kitchen.

Emily moved toward him. "What did he say to you?"

"Nothing," Eddie said. He placed a hand on Emily's back. He hummed from deep in his stomach to try to calm her.

"Tell me what he said."

"I don't want to talk about it," Eddie said, moving his hand up and into her hair. Emily pulled away. "Tell me."

He shook his head. Emily saw the deep circles under his eyes and that he hadn't changed clothes since yesterday.

"I don't know. Crazy stuff."

"What was that?" Emily thought she heard a hand on the door and a breath against the screen.

"Wind," Eddie said.

She covered her eyes with a hand.

"You know, with my friends it's their mothers that worry about them," he said.

"I worry about you," Emily said.

"Then why do you do shit like this?"

"You know I didn't do this." She motioned to the tattered room.

Eddie stared at her. She saw that he was shaking, and she reached for him, but he slipped away and walked to his room. She heard the door shut, then lock behind him.

Emily went to the door and cupped a hand to listen. "Come out," she said. "I want to talk to you."

"No, I won't," he said.

Emily went into her bedroom and lay in the dark. She heard muted sounds through the wall. *Quiet,* she said, *quiet.* And then carefully she began to plan. No matter how boyish their lips looked in the hot sun at the beach, or how bad the feeling got of wanting a stranger, from now on she would choose only one. Every day she'd pick a Bible verse. *Start now,* her mind stomped out. From near the bed she picked up the Bible and flipped through, trying to find her fate in the rice-paper pages. *He turneth the rivers into a wilderness, and the water springs into dry ground.*

Eddie opened the door and walked to the bed, brushed hair away from her face, took the Bible from her hands and set it on the side table. "You pushed him too far," he said, his voice as clear and deep in the dark as a lover's.

Emily turned from the image of herself in the bar mirror. "You alone?" the tourist said, his hairy hand resting on the bar, on one of his fingers a square ring with a too-big-to-be-a-diamond stone in the center.

"I'm waiting for someone," she said and walked to the bathroom. She'd stopped at Paolo's for a drink on her way to Birdflower's. The light and chatter from the bar had drawn her over. In the stall she leaned forward, not letting her thighs touch the seat. She rinsed her hands in the sink and ran her wet fingers through her hair.

She came out, sat down, and watched a few couples dance drunken and awkward. There was a man with white blond hair sitting alone. She posed her hips forward so he could see better and slowed her eyes, let them take in all but him, looked at him as though he was any other detail, then gazed back to the dancers. Quickly, he was up and coming to her. Lanky build, narrow hips, awkward swagger. He smiled in an offhand way and asked her name. She told him and then he asked if she was married.

"I was," she said. "But it turned out bad."

The man's arm brushed her shoulder. She backed from him, nearly dropping her beer, and walked barefoot out of the bar.

The rain was light but steady. She walked along the road on the broken yellow line. It was as if some giant needle had seamed up the soundside and the beach, and carefully, heel to toe, she followed the stitches toward the murky signpost.

Usually she tried not to think about that night she left Daniel. But it was impossible now. Slowly, as the seasons change, as snow gathers on the highest Tennessee mountains, a restlessness had come over her. A hurried feeling in talking to Daniel and even sometimes a carelessness in handling Eddie. It seemed as if the floor of the house began to tilt backwards. Now it was obvious that she should have told him, that maybe together they could have figured it out. But instead she started to go to Nashville on Saturdays. She made up excuses about shopping, about doctor appointments, about lunches with old friends from high school. She found bars: the Blue Note, the 1000 Club, one called Dover's. It never took more than an hour for her to pull some man over. She'd start a careless conversation with them, let her knee slant toward theirs, and listen to their stories. She fell into them gradually. The first few Saturdays she'd left the bar early, insisting that she had to get out to her parents' house in the country. Then after a month of teasing, of trying to figure out what was happening and if it could be remedied by simple attention, a shy man had come along. He was like the blond children in Christmas pictures. Drunkenly they undressed each other as slates of sunset fell through the hotel blinds.

This became her way then. There were moments of remorse: while bathing Eddie, she caught her eyes in the medicine chest and thought, *How can I do this?* Once, sorting through old photographs of her wedding, her stomach had clenched and she'd felt dizzy. Often on Mondays she'd swear to herself that this weekend she would not go. But on Saturdays she would drive to Nashville.

It was unclear who had finally told Daniel. He accused her and immediately she admitted—not to all, but to one man. She created him by combining all her favorite qualities from each. One's fragile scent of mint and wool, another's chest, one's lovely pale body hair, the fingerlet curls from another, one's pondish-green eyes, and another's cowboy thinness. It did seem, even to her then, like a single man.

Daniel had silently taken the bottle down from a high shelf. "Do you love him?" he said. "That's all I want to know."

Emily tried to answer honestly, to piece together all those afternoons. The details slipped away like water into the ground and Emily felt as if she too was somehow evaporating. *Yes*, she said. Not because it was true, but because she knew it would give her a foothold in whatever came next.

Now she'd come to the highest point of the ramp and looked out to the dim shore. No moon. Just a million pinpricks of light.

She heard the roar of water and felt wind mixed with rain against her skin. She turned her back and walked quickly off the ramp and started to run in what felt like long elegant strides up the beach highway.

Their cigarette tips glowed, moved up to their mouths then down as they sat in bed against the cool wall in Birdflower's cottage. Emily said, "It's always been like this: from one bed to another."

Birdflower took a drag. "Does he have a gun?"

Emily felt the heat and closeness of his legs. "I don't know," she said, tipping her ashes over the side of the bed. "He's not what I knew." She flinched at the sound of a car's tires and then saw the lights flash quickly over the wall. "I'm sorry," she said, pulling hard on the cigarette, trying to make herself, the bed, and the room all into smoke. Her spine was getting sore against the headboard so she slipped down under the sheets. "I have things to think about," she said, pressing her head to the pillow.

Birdflower looked down at her. "So do I," he said.

"This is me," she said.

"I know." He let his fingers brush her shoulder.

"You'll never know everything," she said.

"I don't need to know but so much," Birdflower said.

"There are things—"

"I don't care," he said. "Just tell me if you feel like doing it with anyone else." He rubbed his eyes and tipped his head back to the wall. "I might hurt you."

"No, you wouldn't," she said.

"We've been up too long," Birdflower said. "I don't even know what I think."

"The light will help," Emily said. "Everything will change then." She saw a big pink shell on the rag rug. She held it to her ear. "Do you hear me?"

The ocean roared and she pressed the big shell into her temple

—she knew the trick; her own pulse magnified in the caverns of the conch shell.

Ten years was a long time, especially on an island like this one. She was familiar with the seasonal routines. Summer heat's steady work, the pause and seep of fall, cedars sculpted by winter, then spring's rustling pulse and the peeling back again to summer. Each had its own grooved ways, familiar as sisters to her. And this was the first time—besides that December years ago when a man had offered to take her to Barcelona—that she had tinkered with the thought of leaving. She knew John Berry never went farther than Norfolk. Emily watched the bars of light on the ceiling; she shook her head.

Anywhere it would begin again. She held the shell close to her ear and after another hour or so, at the first rise of gray light, let it lull her to sleep.

AUGUST

Let's ride a gull's wing. First in the direction of an August moon, then rounding back attracted by movement somewhere in the valley between dunes. It's a nude couple on a white sheet that whips up and molds around them. The man lets his hand rest on her stomach and watches for falling stars; the sleeping woman dreams of the sheet lifting, floating them over the water as if they were some great bird. The man pulls her close. From this vantage, high over the water, the moon is ahead, and the embracing couple hold light like a lantern.

FOURTEEN

LILA'S WORRIED

L ila imagined being inside of herself, watching her tiny baby opening its mouth to the size of a grain of sand, then wider like a penny, a quarter, a rubber ball, a Frisbee, Hula-Hoop —Lila felt her hands go up and a pull at her fingertips. The mouth still opening, the swamp ponds, the round inlet, and then the whole night sky as she watched her feet disappear into the baby's mouth.

"I'm still talking to you," her father said as she held her fork, peas quivering, in front of her mouth. "Don't get your heart all sick over that boy."

Lila chewed and watched her father push his chair back. Her father looked like a piece of beef jerky from being the focal point of the sun on his boat for so long. His skin was hard and thick, especially on his forehead and at the top of his shoulders. He was skinny, too, and Lila attributed this to drinking whiskey and waking so early every day of his life.

"You tell her," he said to Lila's mother, who stood scraping a plate into the garbage, her housedress moving about her knees.

"No use," she said, not looking up. "Love is blind."

"And deaf too," Lila's father said.

Lila watched a thin version of her father's face in the knife by her plate and phrased the way she would tell Eddie tonight. They would sit on his stoop in the light of the porch lantern and she would say it right out, each word solid as apples lined up on a kitchen counter.

"You meeting him tonight?" her father asked, getting up. He spun a toothpick between his teeth.

Lila nodded her head and said in a French accent, "Of course, Papa."

He shook his head and moved to the screen door. "It's not all as great as it seems now from your angle," he said.

"I'll be the judge of that," she yelled after him. She heard him settle himself in a porch rocker.

Alone at the table, Lila sipped milk from a beer mug. She was five days late. In the bathroom, twenty times a day, she would kneel on the cool blue tiles, make promises, and ask for favors. "I'll become a nun," was the latest. "I swear I will," she'd whisper to the toilet seat, clenching the shag lid cover with both hands. Lila pushed the pork chop bones around and made a cross. She saw herself like Julie Andrews in *The Sound of Music.* In black robes, her head bowed to the rail, she would hear the voices of children chanting in a low, holy way behind her. Then a sound like the pump of birds' wings and she would turn her head to the

stained glass window, to the blue sky above that, and thank him
for taking it back.

Lila's mother came from the sink and put her fingers in Lila's
hair. "You look tired. Why don't you go lay down?" she said. Lila
thought maybe she'd go with him to Tennessee, move right into
his room—sleep curled around him in between football sheets.
Every day her belly would balloon until her stomach was between
them like a hard, round basketball. When her time came, she
would know and rise early to walk through his father's field of
seedlings.

"I remember my first one," her mother was saying. "His name
was Dean. He scooped ice cream at the stand they used to have up
near the beach road." Lila watched her mother's body expand
with breath. Her face was still flushed from leaning over the dinner pots and her hair was sloppily knotted at the back of her head.
"He told me about the lizards and cactus they had in New Mexico."

"What happened?" Lila said, hard-pressed to believe her
mother had ever had a teenage boyfriend.

"Not much," her mother said, moving back to the sink's running water. "After the summer I got a few letters talking about the
desert, but he never invited me."

"You wouldn't have gone anyway," Lila said.

"Who knows," her mother said.

There was a thought: She could hitchhike West, a cigarette dangling from her bottom lip, red bandanna around her neck, always
resting in the shade of a big cactus, using the tumbleweeds for a
bed. Maybe get a job in one of those gas stations two hundred
miles from nowhere. She could walk out into the desert and have
her baby in the warm sand.

Lila set her plate near the sink where her mother was rinsing
dishes. She walked down the hallway and flopped across the bed.
The white furniture still held light in the early dusk. She stared
dreamily at the map above her bed, blurred her eyes, then closed

them so the shapes of the map were emblazoned on her inner eyelids. There were places where no one would find her, Borneo, Madagascar, Sudan. After it was all over she would come home, her sack of trinkets jingling on her back and her hair shortish like the lady explorers' she'd seen in books.

Lila heard her father humming on the porch and her mother opening cupboards to put away dishes. Maybe she would stay with her parents and hide it. Always wear big blouses, and eat dough-nuts and brownies in front of them. She would only whisper to Birdflower. Then he'd help her carry the frozen beef patty boxes. He'd rub her ankles. She'd go alone to a spot on the point, wedge herself into a crevice, grab onto the big rocks, and push till the baby slid out and plopped into a saltwater pool with grayish-blue starfish cleaving to the bottom. The baby would breathe in water, smiling from under the surface at her, and swirl through the nar-row mouth of the pool out to sea.

Her mother and father were whispering about her on the porch. They always had ideas on what she should be doing. Lila remem-bered when her mother told her to pay attention to the dark McKin boy, to Jacob Whitney, the son of the coast guard captain, and to thin Matt Lumly, because she would have to choose from these. Her mother said to notice their temperaments, how they handled the few dollars their parents gave them. Lila stared. "Do you really think I would marry one of those idiots," she said. Her mother started to cry. But Lila didn't care. No one would force her to marry a stupid fishy island boy.

Lila hung her head over the edge of the bed. She could still hear her parents on the porch. A tiny beige arm stuck out from under the white ruffle of the bedspread. She smacked the doll under the bed, rolled over on her back, and watched the shifting willow leaves speckle shadows over the room's walls.

Things women did stayed with them. Like having abortions, like losing their virginity, like Eddie's mother: no one on the is-land forgot the things she did. Even Lila would sometimes look at her on the beach in her bikini and imagine the men she'd been with standing around her.

Lila went to the closet and picked out a blouse to wear, one she had ordered from a catalogue. The blouse had real gold threads running through it that glittered in the darkening room. She put her hands to her waist and stuck out her chest to admire her lean body. She ballooned her stomach, then contorted it all out and arched her back. "That's what you'll look like," she said out loud into her twinkling blouse. "Like a fat old cow." Lila made her face look serious. She saluted her image. "Good luck," she said, then ran out of the house, speeding in a line to her bike leaning against the porch.

"Be back by eleven," her father yelled after her.

Her hair flew back and she took her fingers from the handle-bars. She knew this was like flying and that birds didn't have it any better. She passed the lighthouse, rounded the inlet, sped by the Trolley Stop and the gas station. She turned down Eddie's street and pumped hard on the pedals until her front tire slammed into sand. She got off then and walked her bike.

Daylight was nearly gone and the moon was clouded to a puzzle piece. Faintly, she saw Eddie in a white T-shirt throwing pebbles into the yard. His arm slung sideways. He pitched each stone as if it might skip in and out of the grass. The arcing arm movement let Lila see the scene clearly: herself at the kitchen table and the baby staring at her from a bassinet, watching her face as she took a long swig of a beer. In front of Eddie's house she pushed her kickstand down and watched the metal rod sink into soft sand.

FIFTEEN

TALL BOYS

Ultimately, in relationships," Neal said as he turned the Dart onto the highway, "everyone is selfish."

"I don't know," Eddie said.

"This is how I figure it. A person gets bored with their life in general. Not with their lover, wife, or husband. And the cheapest, easiest thing to do is have an affair."

"I couldn't tell you any of that stuff," Eddie said as his hand snaked up and down in the wind out the window.

The cook looked at him. "How many beers do you want for you and your little friend?"

"A six is fine," Eddie said, reassured that Neal remembered the point of the drive.

"You *will* drink a few with me first?"

The Dart passed a kid pushing his bike on the soft sand shoulder. Eddie was uncomfortable. "Sure," he said. "But I gotta meet her at midnight."

"Great," Neal said, adjusting the radio. "We'll cruise a little."

Eddie dropped his cigarette out the window and looked down to see the smattering of sparks. Since she had touched the inside of his wrist—whispered it so close to his ear he had heard each nuance of her breath—all he had thought about was Lila being pregnant. The fact made everything seem too loud: people's voices, the ocean, the dishwashers at work—the volume made him sick to his stomach and he couldn't forget it, not for one second. Though he had promised not to, he wanted to tell, to spread it over as many people as possible so that his solid problem would thin out and begin to disintegrate like an aspirin melting in water.

Eddie saw Neal looking at the crotch of his pants. Earlier, at work, while sorting silverware, he had noticed Neal staring at his rear. His mother had assured him that Neal would never actually touch him. But still. He'd heard from friends about the queer swim team manager who after meets stared through the steam into the shower room. He worried that the guy at the gas station would see him waiting in the car when Neal sashayed in to get beer. All I need is for people to talk. His eyes teared and he kept saying just under his breath: *It would be stupid to cry.* Neal hummed with the radio. "Do you have dreams about her?" he asked. "Nowadays I only dream about men."

Eddie thought Neal inched his hand across the front seat, but he didn't want to act as if he'd noticed.

"Can't we get the beer," Eddie said.

"In a minute," Neal said, driving toward the docks. "Tell me what it's like."

Eddie thought his mouth smirked slightly as he made a U-turn in the dock lot. "You know what it's like," he said.

Neal gave a snort. "I guess I do."

They rambled back around the inlet. Eddie slumped against the door and thought of getting so drunk his mind would move without his willful force from one thing to another. Neal pulled into the Texaco. "Tall boys?" he burlesqued. Eddie nodded and watched Neal walk in and get beers from the glass case. He didn't want to quit high school and come live here. Those deep lines would form around his eyes from squinting all day against sun and water. Eddie tried to imagine himself as a fisherman, guts smeared on his T-shirt and his beard uneven as a rag. His foot kicked the bottom of the glove compartment. But if he brought her home, his father's face would redden and he'd call him out to the barn, asking intimate and embarrassing questions.

His stepmother would put bushels of peaches in front of Lila and have her peel them and then stir till her fingers were sore from moving the big wooden spoon in the huge pots past dusk and into the dark.

Neal got in and shut the door. "You got some time," he said. "Let's cruise to the beach and drink a few."

"Okay," Eddie said. "But I got to be there by midnight."

"Kind of a late date," Neal said. He looked over his shoulder and backed up the Dart.

"Yeah," Eddie said. He rolled his hand to a fist and dug his nails into his palms. Once, while in the bathtub, through the cracked door, his mother had explained how a lover had never come along who treated Neal well and how, as a child, he'd been beaten up regularly for being a sissy. Eddie had sat at the kitchen table listening to his mother explain that Neal had told her he never knew his father and only remembered the broad brim of his brown hat and the calloused upper palms of his hands. Still, Eddie squirmed: *No matter how lonely the guy was, how hard his life had been, he better not try some move on me.*

As the car lumbered up the wooden planks of the beach ramp, Neal said, "You're not talking much."

Eddie popped a beer; it foamed up and he took a gulp.

"Your mother told me the whole story," Neal said.

"He won't be back," Eddie said, jolting forward as the car's wheels fumbled over the sand. He didn't want to talk about John Berry's break-in.

The car stopped, they both settled silently into the dark. The cook lit a cigarette and popped a beer for himself. Eddie swigged his down fast, tossed the empty to the back, and opened a second. This is helping, he thought. This is definitely helping. A few gulls swooped in front of the crescent moon.

"My mom, you know, shouldn't do a lot of the stuff she does," he said.

"She just comes and goes," Neal said. "I understand it. Like I said, life gets dull."

Eddie watched Neal's cheeks hollow as he dragged on his cigarette. His hair, a brushcut with loose longer curls in the back, was cool. He does it with boys, Eddie thought. He remembered himself staring at his gym teacher back in junior high. Eddie'd daydreamed that during warm-ups Mr. Graudins came over and kissed him right on the lips while the other boys kept counting their sit-ups in one thunderous voice. It must have been some kind of mistake. Because he liked girls. Just the sight of one sometimes turned him on. He was getting hard now thinking of the way Lila threw back her head and twilled her throat like a bird.

Odd things could get him going: certain wrestling holds, advertisements, the jagged movement of the school bus—even the slight wrinkles around the eyes of older women.

Neal reached for another beer. "Does she suck you?"

Eddie's eyes pooled. He would slam the door and run into the surf, swim so hard he'd quickly be a mile out in the dark ocean. "Stop talking about her," he said fiercely.

"I'm sorry," Neal said. "I thought you might want to talk about it or something."

Eddie wiped his eyes with the backs of his hands. *What a crybaby.*

"She's pregnant," he said, the fact out there and living in the air before he could even reconsider. The ocean waves beat back and forth against the sand.

"So that's it," Neal said, stretching his legs to the brake pedals. "What are you going to do?"

"We're talking about getting married."

"That's no good reason to get married."

"I can't think of anything else," Eddie said.

Neal put a hand on Eddie's shoulder. "I'll lend you my car," he said. "You can go to one of those clinics in Norfolk." He moved closer. "You can have your life just the way it was gonna be." Neal leaned his head on Eddie's shoulder.

"I have to be there *now,*" Eddie said.

"Okay, baby," the cook said, and as he lifted his head, he rested a dry kiss on Eddie's neck.

The car moved backwards, then forwards toward the ramp.

Eddie held the brown bag to his face and blew his nose.

"These next few nights I'll leave the keys right under the seat," Neal said.

He drove around the inlet past the lighthouse and finally pulled onto Lila's road. "Just take it and go."

"Thanks," Eddie said, shutting the door with his back. He walked fast carrying the bag, as though it was a baby, toward her house. His eyes went to the smoky rectangle of her bedroom window. Neal's car did not move. *Go on,* Eddie said, swinging a leg over the low white fence. He creeped up to her window and heard Lila breathing slowly inside. Tapping lightly on the screen, he whispered, "Please come out. Or let me in."

SIXTEEN

FERRY TO SHORE

Eddie sat in the parking lot of the gas station waiting for Lila. Gulls swooped around the Dart and it seemed that just that second the first grayish light was tingling up. Like the beginning notes of a song. Different from the verse and chorus because of a deliberate delicate leisure. He picked at the foam leaking through the front seat. Lila had agreed to meet him at five-thirty. To forget waiting, he tried to figure out what qualities he'd gotten from his mother. He looked like a sliver of her, like a cutting that grew differently in height and shape but still had the same hue. But it was characteristics, not looks, he was concerned with. Unlike his friends, but much like his mother, Eddie knew he cried easily and over things that seemed stupid. Like when his mother said she couldn't go to the beach with him, or worse. In school last fall he got teary-eyed when the coach had told him the new sweats wouldn't arrive in time for the first match.

He watched the sky pause before the sun tipped over the water. His stomach growled and he remembered wrestling season when, to make weight, he'd eaten only apples. He could still see them: the morning one that his stepmother set out on a plate, the lunch apple in a brown bag, then the dinner one, sliced thinly and served in a bowl with a few nuts and raisins while his father ladled gravy over his chicken.

Eddie glanced back and saw Lila far down the road: a dot with a small orange satchel.

He felt for the stiff twenties he'd taken out of the little one-teller bank yesterday, then started the car.

She stuck her thumb out like a hitchhiker as he stopped and threw the side door open for her. Lila put a brown bag by her feet and tipped the orange thing into the back.

"What's that?" Eddie thought that it was a parachute and Lila would want them to throw themselves off the highest building in Norfolk. The single parachute would not be strong enough for both but would let them eye the blue smudge of the Atlantic before splattering them on the asphalt.

"A tent," Lila said.

"I can afford a room," said Eddie.

"Nope," Lila said. "I want to be near as possible to the flat dirt during all this."

He pulled a U-turn and headed for the ferry.

"The cook's wheels ain't bad," she said, leaning her feet up on the dash.

"Did you leave a note?" he asked.

"It's all set. They think we're staying with your aunt."

"My mom wasn't home," Eddie said. He looked down at the gas gauge.

"Figures," Lila said.

"I wish you wouldn't act like that about my mom."

"I think I can say anything I want."

Eddie shook his head and shivered.

"You're cold?"

"No," said Eddie. "I thought of something."

Lila said, "It's impossible not to."

"Not that. Neal made a move on me."

Lila squealed. "What did you have to do to get the Dart?" She pressed an elbow into his ribs.

"Nothing," Eddie said. "Don't be so stupid about it."

"Why?" Lila said. "It's stupid to act so boring and grown-up. We go up there, lay the money down"—her voice thickened—"and it's over just like that."

She turned her face away.

"I'm sorry," he said.

"What do you know?" Lila said, turning on the radio and flipping the dial from station to station.

On the ferry Lila asked Eddie about heart attacks. Last night she had had a dream: first her heart beating fast as a bird's, then she felt it swell and nudge out of her ears and mouth, encasing her body like a giant soap bubble. "Then," Lila said, "like a pin pops a balloon, *bang*. Little pieces of pinkish skin were all over the beach—"

There was a hard rap on Eddie's door; he flinched and saw John Berry's face beyond the glass. He rolled the window down an inch.

"Up kind of early," John Berry said. His hair was long, past his ears and blowing.

Eddie was silent.

He pointed at Lila. "Does your father know you're out here?"

"I tell my daddy everything," she said sweetly.

"Is that right?" John Berry said. "I'd like a word with you alone, Eddie."

"No way," Eddie said and started rolling up the window.

John Berry pushed his hand on the moving glass. "Please," he said. "It's nothing bad."

This will never stop, Eddie thought as he opened the door. Lila grabbed at his shorts. "Everybody says he's a crazy man now," she whispered. He pressed the door shut gently and followed John Berry up the stairs. Eddie pulled the sleeves of his sweatshirt down against the cold. At the top he saw the island's long rows of telephone lines strung like a lizard's spine down the highway.

He opened the door of the wheelhouse. John Berry, with a hand on the big wheel, was guiding the ferry.

"I wasn't thinking right," he said quickly.

Eddie didn't answer.

John Berry turned his head from the window and said, "I've got nothing against you. Never did. You stop seeing in front of you when you're like I was. You only see what plays like a movie inside your skull, showing what you were hoping would happen, and spliced between it, I saw the things I'd heard." He paused to guide the ferry through a pattern of buoys. "I want you to tell her I'm sorry."

"What makes you think she'll listen to me?" Eddie said.

"You're her flesh," John Berry said. "She knows that." He looked at Eddie and then let his eyes fall to his hands. "I need someone." John Berry blushed. "You have to tell her that I'm sorry and that you want her to come back to me."

Eddie said, "If that's what you want, why'd you mess up her stuff?"

John Berry said, "Your mother is the only one for me."

"You know she doesn't have that much," Eddie said.

John Berry clenched his teeth. "I'm trying to tell you something."

"Yeah," Eddie said. "Sure, I'll tell her, if you don't kill her first."

John Berry said blankly, "I need her with me."

Though Eddie would never admit it, he was strangely honored that John Berry would talk to him about his mother. It was as if he'd been asked into their bedroom to moderate. Each would tell his or her side and he'd hold up their words, turn them around, examine them like a glass held to light, and decide one way or the other.

"Want to steer?" John Berry said.

"No," Eddie said, though he could imagine the varnished wood of the captain's wheel under his fingers. "I have to get back to Lila. She's not feeling that great."

"I've seen a lot of girls go over on this early ferry and I'm not so stupid to think all of them are going to the malls in Norfolk," John Berry said. "Is that girl pregnant?"

"Yeah," Eddie said.

John Berry looked over and Eddie averted his eyes to the sea charts on the wall. "Come here and drive this boat a minute," he said. "I got a cramp in my hand."

Eddie walked over and took the wheel.

"Turn a little to the left," John Berry said, pointing over the ocean to the day markers. "Now to the right."

She pulled the flap to enter the tent and lay down in the cool patch of grass inside.

"Well?" Eddie said.

"I have to go over at four. They need to take another test."

"How long does it take?"

"How should I know?" Lila said as she spread canvas flat on the grass and arranged the sleeping bags in one corner. "Can you believe we're stuck between two Winnebagoes? We look like a refugee camp compared to those things." She stared at her stomach. "It's nuts," she continued, placing both hands on her lower belly, "that something could be alive in there."

"It looks like a fish now," Eddie said, flat on his back next to her. Outside, a kid started screaming about dropping his freezer pop.

"What did John Berry say?"

"He wanted me to apologize for him."

Lila turned to him. "Are you going to?"

"That's all her mess," Eddie said. "I've had enough to do with it."

"Your mother sure is something," Lila said. "My mother says people like her because she doesn't care who she's with or what she's doing. Anyway, that's what I overheard her say on the phone."

"Gossips," Eddie snapped.

"Think she'll stay with Birdflower?"

"Maybe. But who knows?" he said. "I've learned there's no telling with her." Eddie heard a slice of cartoons as the door banged on one of the Winnebagoes.

"You don't like her sleeping around, do you?" Lila said. "And I wouldn't either. But I've heard she's slowed—"

"Hey, come on, she's my mother," Eddie said, hands held high in the air.

"Fine," Lila said. "We better get ready." She grabbed her brown bag and left the tent. Eddie followed. Lila was always trying to imply that he was in love with his mother, but there was nothing he could say to convince her that he wasn't.

She stared at him.

"I'll stand outside and wait for you," he said. "And hand you quarters for hot water."

"Okay," she huffed and turned. They walked along the path to the showers. WOMEN in white letters on a green shack, a silver nozzle hanging above. She got in and quickly threw her clothes item by item over the door to him. "Give me one," she said. He held a quarter over the side. She pressed it in and turned the knob. Water beat down and began to puddle on the cement floor and drip down the drain. Eddie saw the pink pads of her feet.

"Do you know what the most beautiful word is?" she asked over the push of water.

Eddie lifted the clothes to his face to smell her.

"Negative," Lila said from behind the door. "Negative."

Of those scattered throughout the clinic waiting room, Eddie suspected three women were there for abortions. One near Lila's age sat with a big storybook Bible on her lap and a boyfriend pointing to a page. The other two were older. Near the front door a black woman read a magazine while her little boy ran a fire truck up and down the walls in a crazy path. And near him, a woman his mother's age sat with a concerned-looking man watching a late afternoon nature show on the waiting room TV. There were others who Eddie presumed were waiting for friends or were here for checkups. Their bodies did not send off that desperate energy that seemed to billow in the air around Lila and the women he suspected.

When the nurse stepped out, shuffling files, Eddie squeezed Lila's hand. The nurse called her name.

"I have to pee in a cup," she said quietly to Eddie.

Eddie watched the door close.

When would they ask him to step forward and lay down the money?

Things were not going well at all. There were just two things he'd wanted from this summer and now both had gone bad. He had not talked to his mother, and sometimes he thought that because he had not done so his mother had had a bottle thrown in her face. And as for getting laid, Eddie thought, looking around the room, just look where it had gotten him.

This summer had flipped him and pinned his shoulders. He was reminded that his mother had told him she'd gotten pregnant the first time she'd had sex. She told him this on his sixteenth birthday, to imply his specialness, but also to show him that his life might be ruled by circumstance and passion. His plans for this summer, he thought moodily, were all fucked up.

The door opened and Lila came out. She sat down next to him and whispered, "I had shy bladder at first, but then it was okay. I looked at the other samples when I sat mine on the testing table. It was the color of the rest. No darker or lighter. I even smelled a few."

"Yuck," Eddie said.

"I'd drink them all if it would do any good," Lila said.

Eddie held her hand. "So we'll know for sure in a few minutes?"

"Yep," she said. "I keep wondering if one of these suckers might have a bomb." She deliberately eyed each face in the waiting room. "Do you think any look like born-again Christians?"

Eddie said, "We can leave if you want."

"No, we can't," Lila said. "Don't be stupid."

"You can change your mind," he said.

"Please," Lila said.

A different nurse came out and called Lila's name. She got up and followed the nurse, who closed the door behind them.

His mother had described to him her light-headed dreams of an oval with a creature rolling and changing like a kaleidoscope inside. But, Eddie thought, there was also something desperate and horrible about a red mucousy thing attaching itself to your innards. Lila hadn't said this exactly, but she had mentioned the weirdness of a creature stealing your food and lounging on your organs as if they were throw pillows. But then he himself had been one of these big-headed little gargoyles. Eddie didn't know what to think. For a moment he thought of himself caught in Lila's body, struggling to grow an arm, then a palm, and finally each thin finger flicking out strong as switchblades.

Eddie tightened his calf muscles and squeezed his fingers

around the arms of the chair as if he were on a roller coaster. It bothered him that he couldn't remember how may wins he had had by pin. He saw each match: the gym, the lights, and himself, inching an opponent's shoulders every second closer to the mat. He stood as he heard a hand rest on the door. Somehow he suddenly knew that it would not happen, that for once luck was on his side.

In the motel, Lila fed quarters into the little box on the night-stand. As the mattress shook, she lay back near the trembling bucket of chicken between them. Eddie ate a thigh and watched television. The bones hit his teeth.

In the room, all dark except for the jump and glow of the screen, Lila said, "So this is the fabulous MTV."

"Admit you like it," Eddie said. "It's impossible not to."

"Tonight," Lila said, picking white meat off the bone with her fingers, "I could tell you I liked anything."

Eddie searched the bucket for another thigh. "Should I try to get beer again?"

"No," Lila yelled above the hum of the mattress. She sat up, then stood on the bed and started jumping. Eddie, distracted from his guitar hero on the screen, watched her slap her palms on the ceiling.

He stood and jumped slowly, more carefully than Lila. The chicken spilled onto the bed and bounced. He flicked it off with his toes. "Watch this one," he said, jumping and dancing to a new-wave song on the TV.

"I love this," Lila said as they grabbed arms and pushed off together. Their hair brushed the ceiling. "No babies in here," she said, and looked around as if it was surprising not to see hundreds of infants suspended in air.

"We're saved," Eddie said like a TV preacher. "Praise the Lord."

"We're young," Lila said, wildly throwing her head from side to side with the music. She jumped high, kicking her bare legs. "And we're free."

SEVENTEEN

THE SHARK

E mily watched Lila walk on the beach. She couldn't remember herself ever looking like that: every part so new and
nested perfectly together. She did remember when her hips
spread, a little with Eddie, but more later. Emily looked over the
length of her body to Lila's feet marching in the shallow waves.

"Want to lay out with me?" Emily called.

Lila looked up and smiled shyly. She swayed her thin hips up
the sand. "Spread your towel here," Emily said. "It'll be fun to
talk to you."

"I like your bathing suit," Lila said.

"This old thing?" Emily looked down at her paisley hip hugger. "I got this before Eddie was born."

"Really?"

Emily nodded.

Lila flipped her towel up like a wing and then let it settle on the sand. She lay down on her stomach with a palm resting under each hip.

"Did Birdflower tell you we work together at the Trolley?"

"Yes," Emily said. "He says he doesn't think you like it."

Lila shrugged. "What's to like?"

Emily dug her feet into the cooler sand below the surface. "Did you get in trouble for missing a day?"

"I'm just decoration around that place," Lila said.

"I used to take off like that," Emily said. "No excuses, no plans. Just drive right onto the highway."

"I'd love to be able to drive," Lila said.

"No need for it here," Emily said, her eyes still closed.

"Yeah," Lila said. "Even if I could, there wouldn't really be anywhere to go."

Emily leaned up on one elbow. "I would have loved to grow up here."

Lila opened her eyes and looked into Emily's face. "Can I ask you a question? I've been dying to ask you this forever."

"Okay," Emily said, looking past Lila's profile and farther down the beach to where an older couple waded in the water.

"Why didn't you just reach up and catch the bottle?"

Emily watched the old woman slowly step back to shore and the man do a sidestroke into deeper water. "Have you ever had a bottle thrown at you?"

"No," Lila said, sitting up. "But it seems like you could've caught it and slammed it back at his truck."

"It wasn't a movie," Emily said, watching the old man grow smaller as he floated on his back beyond the waves. "Imagine if you were riding your bike and your father drove up. You'd take a step forward, wouldn't you? And then what if he threw a Coke bottle hard as he could at your face?"

Lila was quiet. "It's horrible to imagine," she said finally.

"Why do you care about this?" Emily asked.

"I can't help thinking about it, is all," Lila said.

Emily lay back and let the sun ease her. She wanted to explain that more and more often now she thought of John Berry; she liked the way he loved her. You could tell he did by the way he breathed, and by the way his skin prickled when he held her. John Berry slept curled up, his face marked with the light sweat of sleep. He was more instinctual than most men. His moods swayed with warm weather, with heat, the seasons.

Emily saw the old man throw his arms up as if cheering. At first she thought he was motioning to his wife about some sort of sea life, maybe dolphin beyond the wake. But then his head dunked under, and when he came up, his hands waved frantically.

"I think that man's in trouble."

Lila stood up, shielded the sun from her eyes.

Emily started to run up the beach. Her feet pounded the wet sand. The man's hands fluttered madly now and his sharpening face was flushed and contorted. His wife waded out, holding up her yellow shift from the water; she pointed to him and yelled.

Emily told Lila to stay with the woman and then ran into the surf. Her body rippled under a wave; she flicked her feet like fins and pulled herself forward with breaststrokes. She saw the man just beyond the wake and thought of her own aging parents. Her heart beat fast; she could feel her hips and ribs pressing down the water. She rose to the surface and swam quickly to him. He grabbed her, strangling his arms around her like a lover. She let out a chain of silver bubbles.

She wedged her foot against his stomach and pushed hard—his bathing suit went down to his knees and floated gracefully off. She scooted up quickly for air, grabbed him across the shoulder, and settled her other hand on the loose skin of his waist.

They started moving slowly, and after a few yards, the man said weakly, "Underwater you looked like a mermaid."

Emily swam hard, concentrating on the flat of green to be crossed and the beige beach and blue sky beyond it.

Lila emerged from a wave, swam to them, and took the man's other arm. "I can carry him," Emily said.

"But he's heavy," Lila said.

They tugged at the man from each side. Emily thought Lila was purposely swimming too fast and she saw her looking down through the water at the man's body, squinting her eyes to make out the edges of his genitals. Emily swam hard. "Hold your breath," she said each time a wave rose over them.

Their feet touched a sandbank and they moved into shallow water. "Are you okay to stand?" Emily said.

They helped him up the beach. She guessed he was seventy or so and she could tell he was embarrassed. His wife ran to him and wrapped a moss-green towel around his waist. He pulled from them. "I'm fine now," he said and staggered toward his blanket.

Emily lay on her stomach, letting the sun ease and loosen her muscles. She was trying to even her breath and figure out why she felt annoyed at Lila: because she had told her to stay on shore, because she could have been drowned and then everyone would have said it was Emily's fault. She thought how young Lila looked in her bathing suit. Her cheek pressed to the sand, flushed, as she watched the ghost crabs tickle out of holes, then, like tiny race cars, speed back in.

"I'm sorry," Lila said. "If I did anything wrong."

Emily sat up. "I don't know," she said. "I just wanted to save that man myself."

Lila laughed. "Maybe another will go down."

"Yeah, maybe all the men on the island will go out there and I'll save each and every one." She didn't wait for Lila to answer, but got up, walked to the water's edge, and scanned the long line where sea and sky met. *He probably loves this girl,* Emily thought.

"Want to walk down to the kettle," Lila yelled to her.

"I'll take you in the car to get a soda first," Emily said. As she turned and made her way back, she saw Lila looking strangely at her. "You know," she said. "You must be a weird mother to have."

Emily smiled. "You don't have to tell me that."

Lila tipped the Coke can to her lips, then let it bump her thigh as she walked. She was watching Emily move, the way you could nearly see her joints work. The skin on her chest and shoulders was patch-brown and slightly wrinkled. *I'll look like that,* Lila kept thinking, and it was just as surprising as when, years earlier, leaning over her cousin's bathing suit, she'd seen her breasts, pink nipples, like the world's most delicate embroidery.

Sometimes it would occur to Lila that she was more interested in Emily than Eddie. Lila would try to think the way Emily did—about men mostly and always about water. To Lila, Emily's mind was like a light source always shaded, a sheet slung over the window, a towel draped over a lamp.

"Do you like having a kid and all that?" Lila said.

"Sometimes it's good," Emily said. She reached down and poked at shells. "What do you think?"

Lila said, "I wouldn't want to be like my mom or do the things some ladies do."

Emily tied a calico scallop shell to the strings of her bikini. "You don't have such clear ideas of what you like and don't after a while."

"I hope I always will."

"I hope you do," said Emily. Birds pattered in front of them, always flying up a few feet before they passed.

From the corners of her eyes, Lila watched the little tummy that seemed to rest on the elastic of Emily's bathing suit bottoms.

"I think I see a beached fish up there," Emily said. "It looks like a shark."

"I see it," Lila said. She wasn't nervous about being with Eddie's mother now, just a little strained.

They both jogged toward where it lay skewed on the sand.

Lila thought of a time she'd walked with her parents on the beach. It was one of those memories before her fourth birthday when everything came to her as sensation: the wind trying to push her to the wet sand, the waves chasing her, the shells she wanted but was too slow to get before the white water took them back into the sea.

The shark was four feet long and solid like a huge piece of rubber. Its mouth had little sand bugs running in and out, and one eye gazed to the sky.

"Let's roll it over," Emily said, using a piece of driftwood to poke its belly.

"Why?" Lila said. "It's dead."

"Help me." Emily put down the Coke can and pushed against the fish. Lila snuggled her can in the sand and helped Emily heave.

"Eddie used to want to take these beached fish home," Emily said as the fish flopped over, showing a white stomach and pale blue sex parts.

"Think it died of old age?" Lila said.

"I guess so," Emily said. "Do you love my son?"

Lila didn't speak for a few seconds and then said, "I think so." She kicked the shark softly, little taps with the smooth pad of her sole. "What kills me is that life slips off them."

"Yeah," Emily said, kicking the shark hard with her toes. Lila raised a foot, stood on the carcass, and offered a hand to Emily. They balanced together on top of the shark. Lila saw that its right eye was filled with sand. She put her toe near it, and a few grains brushed and drizzled from the bottom lip of the eye over the gray-blue skin.

EIGHTEEN

EARRING

E mily cut the peaches she had soaked in warm water. The skins pulled off easily as a wet bathing suit and she sliced them paper-thin. Holding one in front of the kitchen window, she saw pale orange veins, then laid it over the others which overlapped slightly like fallen dominoes. Each time she touched it, the angel food cake gave off tiny confectionery sugar puffs. The sound track from *Camelot* was on the record player.

She ate another fig from the white bowl. Above all other fruit, Emily loved the ass-shaped fig. The flushed purple-green skin and the inside tentacles, sea-like and sweet. And there was that grainy way it made your tongue feel if you ate too many. She picked them carefully from the tree in the backyard near the fence. Squeezing them just enough to know exactly how ripe they would be.

She hummed the songs with the record and thought of Lancelot and the thin, girlish way she'd always envisioned him. She had a theory that all men were either like the beautiful boyish Lancelot or like Arthur, burly and earthy. The crab bisque steamed dreamily on the stove and the cobia, surrounded by green pepper and mushrooms, was baking slowly in the oven.

Birdflower was coming over and Eddie had invited Lila to dinner. A family occasion, she thought, turning the cake slowly around and admiring it as if she were in front of a mirror in a new skirt. After dinner she had promised to pierce Eddie's ear.

It was August. Soon the cold would be in the late night air and then begin inching its way hourly into the day. Eddie would leave in a week and she would settle back into herself, go into the hibernation that happened to all the island people after the tourist season. It was a gradual seclusion, much like the way the sea edges back to itself at low tide.

Again it would be phone calls, crackling and tentative, Emily telling him island gossip and relaying seasonal scenery details: the snow on the beach, the first spring rustle of young sea oats, the joebells budding near the cottage.

"In Camelot," Emily sang in a high, tinkling voice. "Do, do, do, do," she hummed into the bisque, then wiped her hands, leaving a mark like angel wings on her dark shorts.

At the table, she imagined each person in the place set for them. Birdflower, his clean hair held back by a piece of leather, on her right. Eddie on her left in his jeans and black T-shirt. Lila near him, her fingers woven through his under the table. Emily's eyes clicked to the next spot. She had set one too many places and leaned over the table to sweep up the silverware. John Berry tipped her chin. "What about me?" he said and held his plate up for more.

The needle was hiccuping against the end groove. She removed the record, walked to the bathroom, and pulled off her shirt. Adjusting the nozzle, she tugged her shorts off. Tan lines made her body into a geometrical sculpture. Emily poured shampoo into her hand to suds her scalp. She put her face under and felt the bubbles run out of her hair like a long veil down her back.

There was a hand moving past the shower curtain through the falling water, resting on her hip, then sloping slowly up the curve of her breast. Emily leaned into the hand that went to her collarbone, her neck. The curtain split and Birdflower pulled her head out of the water. His lips tasted of warm sun and tobacco.

She rinsed carefully, sticking her rear into the stream, arching her back, moving so every part got water.

"Get us a drink," Emily yelled. Water beat on the small of her back. She heard the clink of ice, the gulp-gulp of pouring gin, and a knife on the wood block slicing a lime. She turned off the water and pulled a towel into the steamy stall. He handed her a drink and sat on the toilet cover.

"Have you thought about it anymore?" Birdflower asked, mixing his drink with a finger.

Emily let the ice rest against her teeth and took a long drink. She set the glass on the soap dish and swung her hair down in front of her. "Not really," she said, moving the towel over her hair.

"Goddamnit," Birdflower said, standing up, filling the small space of the bathroom. "You go on and on never promising, never setting anything straight."

Emily swung her hair back over her head and reached for her glass. From the kitchen the fish smell moved in and around the bathroom.

He paced in half steps in front of the sink.

"I don't owe you anything," she said.

Birdflower rested his hand awkwardly on a wicker shelf which held powder and perfumes.

"Sit down." With her fingers she worked the leather knot out of his hair.

He held his hands to her hips and pulled her closer, ran his tongue lightly in tiny circles around the fine hairs of her lower stomach. He kissed the curly hair between her legs, each time pulling her closer, moving his tongue back into the soft folds. Emily reached a hand out to steady herself. The room felt as if it were filling with water. She knew only the swirling steam and that one wet place. There was a sudden click in the kitchen as the timer rang out.

Emily sleepily opened her eyes. Birdflower stood. She saw a vine moving in his irises, circling to a wreath around his dark pupils, growing even as they stood, straight profiles in the medicine cabinet mirror, shoulder to shoulder, breath to breath, in the tiny bathroom.

"Should we say grace?" Emily asked.

"Sure," Lila said. "I'll do it." She paused, lowered her head, and quickly chanted, "Rub-a-dub-dub, thanks for the grub, yeaaaaah God!"

Birdflower laughed.

"What?" she said, lifting her hands. "I bet he has a great sense of humor."

"He'd have to," Birdflower said. "If he looks down on all this."

Emily poured wine from a tall thin bottle with nuns whispering on the label. "You guys get one glass, okay?" Emily looked over the fish and cold pasta salad with shrimp and black olives. "You think you might go to Tennessee this winter for a visit?" Emily said to Lila.

"I might," Lila said.

"Your mother may come up to my little house in Michigan this winter for a couple months."

"Nothing's been decided," Emily said. The light in the room was fading. Shadows aged every object. She watched Eddie number the items above the white porcelain sink. He seemed to count the petals of the bluebells in a mason jar on the window ledge.

"So," Emily said. "It's been quite a summer."

Lila said, "They're not much different, one from another."

"I don't know," Eddie said. "To me each one seems to have a personality."

Birdflower nodded. "I'll agree with that," he said, reaching for more fish. "But I guess you'd know better than any of us, Lila."

"Even heaven would get boring after so long," Eddie said.

"This isn't heaven," Lila said. "It's not even close."

"A place is what you make of it," Emily said. She got up, walked to the fridge, and got another bottle of wine.

"Yeah," Eddie said. "Dad's wife has this corny plaque in the bathroom—'Bloom where you are planted.' "

Lila laughed, "That'd be great if we were sea oats."

Emily uncorked the bottle and poured more wine for Birdflower and herself.

Birdflower and Lila rocked on the porch swing, angel food cake and peaches balanced in their laps. Emily stood above Eddie, who sat straight against the back of a wooden chair. "Your father will throw a fit," Emily said, holding an ice cube to his ear.

"Good cake," Eddie said, bringing a forkful up to his mouth.

Birdflower set his plate on the floor and grabbed the guitar leaning against the house. He put his ear close and tuned each string.

Eddie said, "Come on." Emily looked at the top of his head and tried to tell herself this was no different from bandaging his cuts when he was a boy. Emily thought of her fingers slowly moving a straight pin forward. The drops of blood that would gather around the needle and the steadiness of her hand as she waited to see the silver tip from the back side rise out of her son's skin.

Lila said, "Get it over with fast—that's the best way."

"Will you hold the flashlight," Emily said to Lila.

"Maybe we should do this inside," Eddie said, the breeze moving the long hair around his neck.

Lila picked up the flashlight and shined it on Eddie's ear.

Emily pressed hard on the ice, let it drop to the porch, and rocked the alcohol bottle back. She dabbed his ear and the point of the pin.

"Hurry," Birdflower said. "Before the numbing wears off."

Fireflies blinked in the front yard. Emily moved her hand closer; the flashlight made her look like a haunted torturess. She inserted the tip of the pin just as a truck's lights blinked over the porch.

"That's him," Eddie said, jerking his head. Blood quickly gathered on Emily's thumb and forefinger.

"He's not stopping," Lila said, watching the truck rock down the sand road.

Eddie said, "I can't feel anything. Is it done?"

"You moved away," Emily said, pulling the pin back and holding the cotton to his ear. "You're bleeding."

"It doesn't hurt at all; all I can feel are your fingers," Eddie said, just as the high beams of the truck turned again and blinked toward them.

Lila focused the flashlight on Emily's face. "I bet he's going to drive past here all night."

NINETEEN

SUMMER ROOMS

mily gave Lila a chunk of cake for her parents, and after bandaging Eddie's ear, told him he could stay out till 2 A.M. John Berry kept circling. Each time the truck turned, Birdflower looked into the lights. He wanted to protect Emily and would fight if he had to. Finally, she asked him to go. He got up and started pacing. The porch floorboards creaked and she urged him again. "Okay," he said, grabbing his jacket. "I won't stick around if you don't want me." Outside on the walk, he looked meanly over his shoulder and muttered, "I hope you get what you deserve."

She sat down on a porch chair and tried to lock eyes with the truck's lights. It was like looking into the sun. *It has to happen,* she thought. Between two people, things could be bad for months, even years, but there was always one thing that signaled the end, that made any future connection impossible. Sometimes it was violence or burlesquing an earlier time, an encounter that meant something and was important to the beginning of the relationship. For some reason, the bottle wasn't enough.

On his twentieth revolution, he slowed and Emily focused on his face folded into the angles of the dark truck. He leaned out the window. Emily held up her hands to show that everyone had left. He went up the road, rounding again. Soon the truck lights grew brighter and moved to her neighbor's house, her own bent cedars, quick over her bedroom window, and then straight to her. He pulled up the driveway and switched off the lights. The truck hummed down.

For a long moment he sat there looking at her through the windshield, then got out and walked up the stairs.

"I need to talk to you," he said. He leaned back against the porch rail and crossed his arms.

She noticed how long his hair had gotten and that, without her to shave them, the hairs on the back of his neck had grown and curled into ringlets. His body had thinned, and there was a ravaged and bruised look about his mouth.

"All I want to know, I guess, is if you love this guy or not."

"I don't know," Emily said.

"Well, decide," John Berry said. "I'll wait." He walked to the porch swing and sat down. The chain creaked back and forth.

"What do you want from me now?" she said, looking over the yard at the shaded window of the neighboring house.

"What I want is a yes or no answer," he said.

"I never think like that," she said. She looked down to her hands resting in her lap. Her fingers curled toward her palms and she deliberately flattened them. The truth was, it was her moods, tonight, tomorrow, and a few weeks after Eddie left, that would motivate her one way or another.

She stood and leaned against her white porch pillar. "The part I like is when you can still buy the future."

"Buy the future?" John Berry asked.

"Yeah. Because it's easy: an empty house on some street, not a specific one with a guy's lifetime of junk spread out like guts in every room."

"None of this had to happen," John Berry said, shaking his head. "You could have told me anything."

The night breeze was deepening and Emily heard the metal mobile chime delicately.

"You know that's not true," she said.

"It is true, damnit." He pulled at the hair on the back of his head, as if to lengthen it.

"You threw a bottle at me," Emily said, and turned. She shivered and felt goose bumps rise on her legs and arms.

"Emily—" his voice thickened. "I'm sorry."

She walked across the porch. "Look at these," she said, turning her head to show him the scars scattered all over her face.

"It was a crazy thing." He grabbed her hand and tried to pull her down to him. The chair swing rocked jaggedly.

Emily freed herself and stepped back. Even in the dark she suddenly seemed to see everything with perfect clarity—the shingled edge of her cottage, the clay pots of jasmine against it, the glints of light off the chain suspending the porch swing, the railings and the bits of bush that reached through them. And him, in the middle of these shapes and angles of wood, looking at her face, counting the places he'd marked her.

John Berry sat on the floor lighting candles. He moved from one short fat candle to the next. They smelled of honey, elderberry, or lemon. Hot wax gathered in puddles on the floor; flame shadows pulsed and jumped on the ceiling. He found shapes: animal bones, starfish, and whales. The poster women seemed to have joined hands in a circle, showed an occasional lip, earlobe, or thigh. Emily ran the spigot in the kitchen. John Berry surveyed the pans and bowls filled with water and arranged around the whole room. Together they sparked like the sea under light. The water stopped running and she carried two long aluminum cake pans into the bedroom. She moved quietly. "One at our feet," he said, lying longways on the oval rag carpet in the center of the candles. "And the other at our heads."

"Lay down with me," he said. He smoothed his fingers on the inside of her wrist, then outlined her inner thigh. Her breathing changed. "Take your shirt off."

She pulled her blouse over her head in one motion. Her loose breasts swayed. John Berry traced the blue veins branching like delicate road maps. He moved his face down and made his mouth and the movement of his tongue the center of the room.

John Berry unzipped her jeans, loosened her underpants, and with two fingers felt for wetness. Emily murmured. He was distracted again by the wineglass near the curve of her lower back. He reached over, lifted it to his lips, then tossed it into a nearby wooden bowl. Water flew up high and landed in droplets on her back. One wick sputtered, made a noise like a soul lifting from a body, and sent the thinnest line of smoke up into the room.

Emily watched the play of bluing crimson flames from inside closed eyelids. His hands were settling on her hips, every finger sending off silver. There were stretch marks there, like water, peachy currents crossing and connecting, moving under the skin then reappearing. She opened her eyes. The candle wax gave in the way mud does around high rivers and gathered on her wood plank floor. *This shouldn't be happening,* she thought, and pulled herself up. John Berry fell back as she rose. "Come back to me," he said.

"You're just doing what you always do, and so am I."

John Berry sighed.

"Get up and lay on the bed," Emily said. She watched his loose sex darken with shadow as he stood and walked in the thin passage between fire and water.

Emily took a deep breath and blew toward him. The air made everything in her room flicker with liquid light.

"Limitations," Emily said. "I know mine better."

"That's too bad," he said.

"It's not bad. It's okay."

They never touched except for once when he brushed the tips of her fingers with his lips. *This summer is broken no matter what happens now,* Emily thought, very late, as she listened to John Berry's breath widen with sleep. For the first time in a long while she felt *still.* For better or worse, the patterns of the island were taken into her completely now. Emily got up and moved about the room, nudging the water containers toward the walls with her feet. She swayed her hips; her hair twirled out. This night she had returned to herself. Spears of flame and shadow flickered over the walls as she moved, and she confused them into men and women and spirits.

TWENTY

TIDES

The *screen* windows of the restaurant dining room gave a garbled picture of the world outside. *This is like being in a beehive,* Eddie thought, as he sipped champagne and listened to a slow tune called "Almost Blue" that played over the restaurant sound system. The name of the singer eluded him, reminding him that on the island he seldom collected facts as he did in Tennessee. When "Almost Blue" was nearly over, he decided that sad songs were okay on a night like this. The kitchen door swung wide and Neal strutted out with a second bottle of champagne.

"It's all downhill from here," Neal said, holding up the bottle like a trophy.

"God save us," Eddie's favorite waitress said. She sat down next to him and began rubbing hard at her temples, as his mother sometimes did late at night.

Neal poured out the rest of the first bottle and they raised their glasses. Eddie tried to imagine his life at home: what a place was like without a breeze off the water. He watched the waitress tracing a birthmark, one shaped loosely like an S, on her arm. She made a sound like moving water while she did this, and Eddie recognized it was the same sound she made when the boss yelled at her. The dining room screens quivered with cool air. "You go on the 6 A.M.?"

Eddie nodded. "Yep. You know, this year I don't seem as anxious to get out of here."

"It's Lila," the waitress said, looking up. "Will you miss her terribly?"

"Naw," Neal said. "Life goes on—he's not going to hang his head over some girl."

"I think it's sweet," the waitress said. "I remember my first love."

Neal rolled his eyes. "You breeders can certainly get sentimental."

The waitress didn't answer. Lazily, she fingered figure eights over her arm, onto the table, then into her champagne.

Eddie said, "If you'll excuse me."

"Stuff goes right through you, doesn't it," Neal laughed.

The restaurant men's room had blue roosters all over the wallpaper and a basket soap dish. As he peed, Eddie tried to figure out what he should be feeling and how he'd say good-bye to everyone. He thought it was kind of pitiful how Neal always lessened certain moments. You got the feeling that nothing meant any more to him than anything else.

This morning in bed, Eddie was thinking of the lighted buoys bobbing in the channel between Hatteras and Ocracoke, and how much like his annual spring going-away dinner they were. Both marked a path to be navigated: one through a royal blue light, the other by a grilled steak.

Eddie watched the yellow mix around with the flushing water. He'd known for a while that things you didn't know had a way of eating at you, but now he also knew that things you did know could stay with you. In some ways, the things he knew about his mother and Lila and the ways of the island were even more worrisome than the vagueness he'd felt before. He flipped the light and walked back to the dining room.

"Did I tell you," Neal said, "that the other waitresses said they would have stayed, but they had to get back to their fat fishermen husbands?"

Eddie poured. "Dig these things," he said, holding up his plastic champagne glass. "You guys are great."

"I was thinking this is a weird place," Neal said, lighting a cigarette and swishing the bottle to see how much was left. "People never seem to get what they're looking for."

"Same as anywhere," the waitress said.

Eddie said, "But here it's worse, because people expect more. They come here to find answers. Life is supposed to be easier to handle on an island like this one."

"You should be relieved to go," the waitress said. "I know I will."

"You all don't know shit," Neal said; his profile tightened quickly. "This place is a dream in the fall when the days are cool and at night you need just one blanket."

"It's a dream now," Eddie said.

"Yeah," Neal said. "Come December, you'll find some sand in the pocket of a pair of pants you never wear and you'll think about this place."

"Everybody gets nostalgic," the waitress said.

"You act like we don't exist when you all leave. Every day you're gone we get up in the morning. I don't even like the summers really," Neal said. He drank one of the last few swigs from the bottle and passed it to the waitress. He looked at Eddie. "You'll be back here. I can always tell when this island has a hold of someone." Neal drank up what was in his glass. "We better get out of here; the boss could blow in anytime."

"I hope he does come in and see us," the waitress said.

Neal shook his head. "You may be leaving, but I need this job."

Their destinations seemed to rise up, separate and scattered, and for what seemed to Eddie like a long while they were quiet. The waitress passed the last swallow to him. He closed his eyes and gulped, thinking that he knew everything right now.

"This is the last time we'll be like this," Lila said as she settled herself on the linen tablecloth Eddie'd taken from the restaurant. The ends fluttered like moths.

"No way," he said. "You'll come to see me. I'll come down at Christmas. Then we can—"

"You're so stupid." She turned her head away from him, back toward the houselights scattered around the inlet. "You'll never know what I mean."

Eddie felt that warm sensation behind his eyes and knew that he might cry. "How late can you stay out?" his voice rose. Lila moved her face close to his and looked at him carefully. With her fingers she brushed his eyelids to check for tears.

"Not much longer," she said.

Eddie nodded. She put her hand on his neck. "Want a butterfly kiss?" she whispered, and put her eye less than an inch from his cheek. She fluttered her lashes. Eddie closed his eyes—it felt odd, but somehow familiar, like that feeling he had sometimes of wings hidden and moving inside of him.

When she stopped, he leaned up and said, "We could get high. Neal slipped me a good-bye present." He pulled a joint from his back pocket.

Lila nodded. He lit it, breathed in, and passed it to her. She sucked in, then coughed.

"Let me," Eddie said. He drew, touched her lips slowly, and filtered the warm smoke into her mouth.

"I like that," Lila said, turning to watch a slow shrimp boat troll its way into Silver Lake.

Eddie watched the island pass in a long jagged line of beige beach and dark brush from the car window. He had the hopeless sensation that even if he decided now to stay, this summer would be over for him.

His mother, her eyes on the dark road, looked sleepy and blank as cross-country drivers do.

"Maybe one whole year you'll stay with me," she said.

He said, "Maybe I will," though he knew the months were forever delineated and that he was too old for life with his parents to change.

"I got you something," she said. With one hand she reached under the seat and handed him a flat package.

She turned on the car light. The cover was black with millions of white spots and THE HEAVENS written across the top. "I look up a lot here," she said. "You know how it is, wide-open spaces and all that. And I thought maybe if you knew the sky better, if you had a few points of reference, you'd be more likely to turn your head up."

"Thanks," he said, watching his mother's face under the harsh light. "I don't have one for you," Eddie said.

Emily smiled. "I'm the mother, remember?"

"You know, it seems like what's between us doesn't have that much to do with that," Eddie said. "I'll tell you something. Starting this fall, starting now, you've got to take better care of yourself."

Two birds rose from the swamp grass, their wings a smudge against the black sky.

She didn't answer, but she did glance at him, and he noticed how her eyebrows rose slightly and her features had an alert look as if she was seeing something new.

He knew that John Berry and she had come to an understanding of sorts. Eddie set his eyes on the small blue lights at the end of the approaching ferry dock and began worrying about what he'd actually say when they got there.

"How'd it go with Lila?"

"Okay," Eddie said. It seemed as if they shouldn't talk about Lila. He had been unable to say the right thing, and then she had to be in so early. On her porch, she'd said good night without even kissing him and ran into the house. He half thought she'd come back, and he'd stood there a minute or two waiting.

At the docks, his mother stopped the car but left the heater on to warm their feet. It was scrappy down here. A toilet shack, a pavilion with picnic tables underneath, a snack machine that sold moonpies and kettle chips, a Coke machine and a telephone booth, the old-fashioned kind, spots of sandburs mixed with rough yellow grass and a scattering of fishy metalworks. They watched the ferry weave awkwardly forward.

"When you were a baby," Emily said suddenly, "every night after dinner you'd cry and the only thing that made you stop was a drive in the car. Even at the red lights you'd cry. Your father drove and you'd lie between us on a blanket, looking up through the windshield at the sky."

Eddie watched an old scrap envelope topple across the ramp in front of them.

"But it's not a bad thing," she said, turning toward him. "I want you to understand that."

Eddie nodded. "I want *you* to like your life," he said evenly.

Eddie took her hand lightly. He saw the slightly worried set of her lips, the pupils of her eyes milky and anxious in the dark.

"You mean everything to me," she said, running her fingers over his inner wrist.

The ferry backed into the dock. A battered pickup truck pulled onto the nearby shoulder. It was butter-colored and tingled the way shades of white do in the dark.

"That's Lila," Eddie said. The truck was her father's; he'd seen it a million times, but he never thought he'd see her driving it. He couldn't believe it. He let go of his mother's hand and opened the door.

"You came," he shouted over to her. He realized how his voice had risen and he blushed.

"Of course I came," she said, leaning her head back on the rest.

He heard the ferry bump shore. Emily leaned over the passenger seat and shouted out the window, "You want to take him to the bus station?"

"Wait a minute now," he said. His mother's face was shadowed and unreadable in the dark, and he leaned closer.

"I could," Lila called.

Emily said, "Why don't you then?"

"You wouldn't mind?" Lila sounded surprised and she looked at Eddie. He shrugged his shoulders.

"No," Emily said, "I really wouldn't."

Eddie stretched farther through the open window and kissed his mother's cheek. "I'll call you in a few days," she said.

She smiled at him as she started the engine, then she pulled out and followed the tourist cars up the beach road. The sight of her car getting smaller and smaller pulled at him.

"You kill me," he said to Lila. He got in and the truck began to climb the ramp. He felt relieved and happy that Lila had come for him, and he watched her thin fingers curled around the wheel.

"I could take the wheel on the road to Kitty Hawk."

"No, I want to drive you all the way." She looked over at him. "Last night was weird."

Eddie pried one of her hands loose and pressed each fingertip to his tongue.

"What are you doing?"

"Taking your fingerprints in case I lose you."

This was the period to the long rambling sentence of the summer. The dawn. His mother. The starbook. Lila and the truck. All these were packed in behind his eyes. He knew the last thing would be he and Lila soaring down the early morning road. They pulled on and the ferryman secured the big chain at the back. Eddie felt the quick tug off the island and then the first few moments of floating between shores.

His mother had told him a few nights ago that she wouldn't be going anywhere with Birdflower. She'd said she was going to rest for a while. And though he still felt anchored to her, the weight was not half what it had been.

Lila got out of the car. Her hood blew back from her jacket and she held her hands up to the gulls. He watched the many wing tips brush her, knowing they must feel like breath. In this way she was like his mother. They were more alive than most people, and this gave them power to draw things to them. For a moment it seemed the birds would lift her above the ferry. He rested his eyes. And when he opened them, the birds were gone and she was making her way through the pressing wind back to him.

From her car, heading back along the beach road, Emily could see the truck's rear lights as they inched over the ramp onto the ferry. It seemed right that her car and Lila's were bookends to the wide mile of beach and lavender sky.

After he left, her mood always varied; sometimes she was light-headed, other times more somber, even teary. Every year she swam. Last summer there'd been a host of Medusa jellyfish sending off green light. The year before she'd stroked straight out, so far that when she turned, the shore looked like a mirage. Once she tried to stand on a sandbank. Barnacles, like white teeth, cut the fleshy part of her foot and blood dribbled into the sand.

The car passed the campground. Tents and trailers looked emberish and exotic in the dawn. The pony pen clattered by. She pulled over, got out, and walked the path that led to the water. The sea smelled of living things, and it reminded her always of her own scent.

Just above the horizon was a thick purple, and above that, a halo of lemon. She slid out of her loose jeans and pulled her sweatshirt over her head. Her toes made twirling ropes in the water behind her, and when the sea was to her breasts, she dived in. Emily saw dark shapes in the water and thought of the weird fish, sea grubs, and mole crabs that lived underneath. She rolled onto her back. The moon was fragile as a paper nickel and the rising sun sent a snake of light across the water toward her. Nobody swims much past autumn, she thought, but I do.

ABOUT THE AUTHOR

Darcey Phelps Steinke, a 1985 graduate of Goucher College, received her Master of Fine Arts degree from the University of Virginia, where she was also a Henry Hoyns Fellow. She worked briefly at the White House as a congressional correspondent before spending a year studying literature in Ireland. In 1986 she was awarded a Times Inc. Fellowship and has recently been a Wallace Stegner Fellow at Stanford. Her stories have appeared in *The Texas Review, The Greensboro Review, The Crescent Review,* and on National Public Radio. She is currently at work on her second novel.